BEST

Kathryn had been quite happy with her engagement to Northrop, until she found the past catching up with her. And the dream she had of an organised future began to collapse . . .

For my mother

BEST LAID PLANS

BY

ROSEMARY SCHNEIDER

MILLS & BOON LIMITED

15–16 BROOK'S MEWS
LONDON W1A 1DR

First published in Great Britain 1985
by Mills & Boon Limited

© Rosemary Schneider 1985

Australian copyright 1985
Philippine copyright 1986
This edition 1986

ISBN 0 263 75283 6

Set in Monophoto Plantin 10 on 11 pt.
01–0286 – 57191

Made and printed in Great Britain by
Richard Clay (The Chaucer Press) Ltd,
Bungay, Suffolk

CHAPTER ONE

KATHRYN LAWRENCE hummed as she walked slowly across Boston Common and up Beacon Hill carrying the two bags of groceries she had bought for the dinner she was catering that evening. The September sun felt warm on her slender shoulders through the thin navy T-shirt she wore tucked into her comfortable khaki slacks. It was a fine day to be alive.

She gazed up at the trees and the stretch of sky that was visible between brick buildings and thought about how orderly and well everything was going for her, for a change. She could hardly believe that she'd done it—she'd finally found a reliable man.

Kathryn had always admired people who lived well-organised lives, and to her great satisfaction, she was about to join their ranks. In less than a month she'd be Mrs Northrop Davis III, and not long after that they'd be starting a family—she hoped. She was thirty-six years old, and if she ever planned to marry and have a child, she had to do it now. It was long past time she started using her head instead of her heart. Hearts were unreliable, at best.

Only a few short weeks ago she'd gone away on holiday to make her decision about marrying Northrop; and instead, she'd fallen in love with a totally unsuitable man—or at least, for a while, she'd thought she'd fallen in love.

As soon as she returned home, she realised how stupid she'd been; but by then it was too late. She told Northrop she couldn't marry him, and in fairness, she told him why.

But Northrop surprised her. 'All you had was a last

fling, my dear,' he consoled her. 'You mustn't let it interfere with our plans.'

Kathryn couldn't believe his generosity. At first she held out against him, but finally he convinced her that he was sincere. Since then everything had gone more smoothly than she could have hoped.

'You're a very lucky woman, Kathryn Lawrence,' she admonished herself. She'd stopped humming, and her smile had slipped a bit; but she determinedly started up another tune. The sky was blue, the air was clear, and she had everything well in hand.

She adjusted her grocery bags more comfortably in her arms and walked the last few blocks towards her home—a neat brownstone that had been left to her by her grandmother, whom she had loved dearly.

But then she was stopped in her tracks by the voice of her downstairs neighbour, Julia Quimby—who had also been left to her by her grandmother.

'Yoo hoo, Katie, you have someone here to see you.'

Mrs Quimby's greeting immediately told Kathryn that something was wrong. No one in Boston ever called her Katie.

Her brown eyes flew from the treetops to the brick stoop where Julia Quimby stood waving her lace handkerchief as though she were hailing a taxi. Looming behind her, and looking too large and real for the narrow stoop, stood the last man in the world Kathryn wanted to see.

'Oh, no!' A hundred sensations, all of them violent, went through her; and she stumbled on the uneven brick pavement and almost dropped her groceries. This couldn't be happening.

Mrs Quimby made a worried noise, and the man came hurtling down the steps to save Kathryn from falling on her face. 'Hey, steady there, Katie. I meant to surprise you, not cause an accident.' His voice was deep and amused and was directed at the top of her

head as he wrapped his arms around both Kathyrn
and the grocery bags.

Kathryn felt as though she were being smothered by
a bear. She lifted her head, which had been pushed
into the groceries, and muttered into his shirt, 'I'm
OK. Let me go!'

He laughed and released her, but he didn't release
the bags. 'Here, let me take these.'

Kathryn's impulse was to hold on to her groceries as
though they were a lifeline, but she glanced at Julia
and decided that a tug-of-war would be out of place.
Begrudgingly, she let the bags go.

The strap of her handbag had slipped down to her
elbow, and she pushed it back up on her shoulder
while she fought for composure. The man's chin had
loosened a piece of her too-silky brown hair from its
topknot, and she smoothed it back from her brow.

She knew that her clear mobile features revealed her
thoughts much too easily, and she tried to put surprise
and delight into her expression rather than the dismay
that actually filled her at the sight of this man. It
wouldn't do to let Julia Quimby know that anything
out of the ordinary was going on.

She gave him a smile that Shirley Temple might
have envied and said brightly, 'My goodness. Hello,
Nick. I didn't expect to see you here.' She made the
understatement of her life. She'd had every reason to
assume that she'd never see Nick Varganin again.

She turned to Mrs Quimby and improvised, 'This is
Nick Varganin, Julia. He's an . . . um . . . old friend of
mine and a new . . . er . . . customer. I meant to give
him a copy of my menu, but I must have forgotten.'
She gave Nick a sidelong glance to see if his
expression might be denying her words, but he was
blandly smiling up at the tiny, white-haired lady on
the stoop.

Julia Quimby, in her turn, was giving Nick an

approving look from his slightly mussed dark-blond hair, over his wrestler's shoulders, which were encased in a well-worn brown corduroy jacket, to the plain brown shoes on his large feet. 'Mr Varganin and I have already introduced ourselves,' she said rather smugly. 'But you know, my dear, I almost didn't know who he meant when he asked for Katie Lawrence. I've never heard you called Katie before.'

Kathryn was momentarily nonplussed for an answer, but Nick was faster. 'All of us fellows called her Katie in high school,' he said heartily. 'I hadn't realised she'd stopped using the name. We haven't seen each other in years, have we, Katie—I mean, Kathryn?' His smile had turned into a teasing grin. Unlike Kathryn, he was enjoying himself.

Kathryn stopped him with a quelling glance. She didn't think she'd ever heard the word 'fellows' said aloud before, and they hadn't called the private academy she'd attended 'high school'. If he kept it up, Julia would be sure to catch on.

'Those bags must be getting heavy and there's ice cream in one of them,' she said quickly. 'Shall we go up to my apartment and I'll get that *menu* for you?'

'Oh yes, the *menu*.' He gave Mrs Quimby a wink and Kathryn wanted to kick him.

She led the way into the house past the kind but nosy elderly lady and then up the stairs to her first-floor flat. The house stood four storeys high including the basement, with Julia occupying the two lower floors and Kathryn the upper floors and roof garden. It was the same arrangement Julia had had with Kathyrn's grandmother, and Kathyrn had never seen any reason to change it. Julia Quimby's grandmotherly interest in Kathryn had never been irksome—until recently.

Now, as she walked up the stairs ahead of Nick, she was acutely aware of the fact that Julia was watching them and Nick was watching her. She could feel his eyes at her back and it made her stiffen her spine. She didn't know how he had found her, but she had to get rid of him before he spoiled everything for her. He might think this was a game, but he was playing with her life!

In her agitation, she fumbled with the key in the lock, but Nick made no comment other than to whistle tunelessly under his breath as he shifted the grocery bags higher in his arms. When she finally got the door open, he stepped ahead of her and his tuneless whistle changed to one of appreciation as he looked around the room. 'Very nice. Very nice, indeed. These old places can be gloomy, but you've opened it all up into one room. I like that.'

Kathryn couldn't help being pleased at his praise, but she refused to let herself show it. She'd had the whole space converted into one large area supported by beams. The living, dining, and kitchen sections were open to each other and separated only by the placement of furniture and colourful scatter rugs over the thick wall-to-wall carpeting. Everything was done in earth tones with an occasional blue or orange accent. The whole effect was one of openness and comfort.

Nick carried the groceries to the butcher-block counter and then turned to smile at her. 'You do a good job decorating, Katie.'

'My name is Kathryn,' she said evenly, ignoring the compliment. *I won't let him get to me. I won't let him get to me*, she told herself.

'Oh yes, Kathryn. Old high school habits die hard.' His chuckle was knowing and, to Kathryn, very aggravating.

She didn't bother to answer him, but shut the door and leaned against it as she watched him wander around her flat, as though his appearance on her doorstep were the most natural thing in the world.

She'd thought she'd begun to forget this great barrel of a man who had told her that his physique had come down to him from generations of Russian peasants. Certainly nothing about him denied his claim that his grandparents had fled the Tsar before the revolution. He had a high forehead, thick dark-blond eyebrows over observant blue eyes, high cheekbones, and too large a nose and mouth.

She remembered telling him that he had a grin like a wolf, and he'd laughed and said that some of his peasant forebears had been Cossacks. Now he was prowling around her apartment like one of those wild and woolly ancestors looking for spoils, and it was up to her to make sure that she wasn't one of them.

'How did you find me?' she asked coldly. She had to let him know immediately just where he stood with her—which was nowhere.

'Now is that any way to treat an old school chum?' he asked with a wounded air. He came towards her, but she eluded him. The same trait of aggressive playfulness which had attracted her only a few weeks ago was a danger to her now.

'That bit about high school was your story, not mine,' she reminded him. 'You have no right to be here.'

'I came up to get a *menu*, remember? That was *your* story.' He looked her up and down and seemed to be amused at what he saw.

Kathryn knew that her cheeks were flushed and her eyes were glowing too brightly, but it was in annoyance, not pleasure that he had come. He'd told her she was beautiful, but she hadn't believed him. She was not aware of how the fine planes and angles of her face came alive when he was around.

She went over to her desk by the living-room wall and opened the right-hand drawer. 'Here's your menu, then. Now you can leave.' She held out the neatly typed sheet of paper and was proud that her hand was barely shaking.

But he had gone over to peer into the grocery bags. 'What have we got here?' he asked.

'It's none of your business.' Kathryn felt a flush of annoyance as she put down the menu and strode across the room to grab the bags away from him. 'I don't know how you found me, but I don't want you here. I thought it was understood that we weren't going to see each other again. You said you were going back to California.'

Her voice had trailed off into a wail, and she had to stop and get herself in hand. She put the bags back on the counter and repeated more calmly, 'I thought you were going back to California.'

'I did,' he said easily, either unaware of her growing desperation or ignoring it. 'The trouble is, I missed you so much I just had to come back east and search Boston until I found you. I should think you'd be flattered.'

'Well, I'm not.' Kathryn didn't believe him for a minute. She turned her back on him and began to rummage noisily in the bags for the ice cream.

She found the carton and then was startled into dropping it as she felt his hands slide around her waist from behind. She swung around within the circle of his arms and tried to push him away. 'Don't you touch me!'

But he didn't release her. 'Don't touch you? When all I've dreamed about for the past few weeks has been doing this?' He pulled her towards him and bent to kiss her.

She moved her head and his kiss landed on her ear, but he began to nibble that and then let his kisses trail down her neck to her throat.

She gave a hard shove against his shoulders which did not break his hold on her; but it did stop his nuzzling at her neck. He raised his head and looked down at her reproachfully, 'Ah Katie, would you deny a dying man a crust of bread?'

'If you're hungry I'll make you a sandwich,' she answered shortly. 'Now let me go!' She pushed against his chest with splayed fingers.

His arms loosened until his hands were again around her waist, but rather than release her, his fingers began a massage of her lower back that he knew drove her wild.

'You can't have forgotten so quickly how good we are together,' he said persuasively.

Kathryn hadn't forgotten a thing—no matter how hard she'd tried—and now she shut her eyes to try to block out the sensations he was reawakening in her in spite of all her resolutions to the contrary.

Kathryn, he'll love you and leave you, just the way he did on that island. Don't let him do this! she cried inside.

She opened her eyes and said, 'No, Nick, not again. What happened between us wasn't right. You can't——' But his head was once more descending towards hers and she couldn't seem to move.

'Wait . . . no . . . this isn't . . .' she said against his mouth. But her attempt to speak only opened her lips to his invasion and then words became useless. She pushed once more futilely at his chest, but he was too strong and the memory of what had happened between them was stronger yet. The taste of his lips and the expert movements of his hands over her body were like a remembered melody.

Kathryn had dreamed of Nick many times since they had parted—longing, unwelcome dreams that left her full of an aching desire she couldn't control.

She felt herself responding to his touch, and she told herself, *Just one kiss. I can give him just one kiss.*

But she underestimated the strength of their mutual desire. Their kisses deepened and Nick pulled her against the solid length of his body. The contrast between her own slender shape and his wrestler's physique had fascinated her from the start. He was unlike anyone she had ever known.

Her breasts, of their own accord, pushed into his chest, longing for the remembered feel of his smooth, almost hairless, skin against her own. Nick sensed her need and his hands slid beneath her shirt and smoothed along her back until his fingers found the clasp of her bra and released it. He slipped her T-shirt over her head in one deft movement and then knelt and buried his head between her small, firm breasts.

Kathryn shut her eyes and pushed against his head, but he only moved lower to the slight mound of her stomach above her slacks. His tongue traced a circle around her navel.

Kathryn felt every bit of her willpower slip away in a haze of desire that sent her dreaming back to her holiday cottage on Block Island and the remembered sensations of their lovemaking. A buzzing noise began to sound in the room, but at first she was no more aware of it than the noise of the traffic out on the street.

It was Nick who finally lifted his head and asked, 'Isn't that coming from your stove?'

Kathryn came out of her haze and realised that it was the oven clock that was making the sound. She'd set it earlier to warn her when it was time to start the rice for the meal she was catering that evening. She always forgot the rice unless she set the timer.

Reality penetrated her awareness like a knife, cutting away the illusion she'd let herself slip into and making her remember exactly who she was. She pushed Nick away and retrieved her T-shirt from the counter where it had landed. Block Island disappeared, and she was back in her proper Beacon Hill flat, saved only by the bell from doing something she would have been very sorry for later.

She kept her back to Nick as she pulled her shirt over her head and walked to the stove to silence the buzzer. 'It's my rice,' she mumbled self-consciously. 'I've got to start my rice.'

Nick didn't reply. Kathryn put up shaky hands to fix her hair and, out of the corner of her eye, she could see that he hadn't moved from the spot where they had been making love. She knew without looking that his lips were curved in a mocking smile.

He'd worn the same smile after the first time they'd made love. Kathryn had been shocked by her actions, and she'd tried to retreat from what they had done together; but he hadn't let her. Again and again he'd managed to return her to the elemental woman only he had ever brought out in her.

But this time it wasn't going to work. They were not at the beach, and he was not in control.

She leaned against the stove and said steadily, 'I have a meal to make. Would you please go away? I don't want you here.'

'You can't expect me to believe that,' he said, beginning to move in on her again. 'You want me as much as I want you.'

Kathryn opened her mouth to dispute his claim, but then she thought better of it. Denials would get her no where. What she needed was cold, clear logic. She cleared her throat and said, 'That may be true—I won't even bother to argue—but it doesn't make a bit of difference. This isn't a holiday any more and it's not Block Island. I have no room in my life for some big wolf of a man who is just passing through.'

'Even when that wolf makes you feel like this?' Nick gave her a knowing look and reached out to take her in his arms again.

But Kathryn put up her hands as though she thought he might attack her. 'Don't touch me. I mean it this time. Don't come near me.'

The panicky ring to her words stopped him. He backed off and said easily, 'OK. Calm down. I won't touch you. I'll even go away if you convince me that it's what you really want.'

Kathryn knew she'd almost lost control again, and she looked away stubbornly as she said, 'I don't have to convince you of anything.'

'Not even to get rid of me?' His smile was insufferably superior and it began to get on her nerves.

'My private life is none of your business or anybody else's,' she stated flatly.

But her words didn't worry him. He snorted a little and said, 'So I've noticed. The whole time we were on the island together you avoided the subject. You told me about your past—your jobs, your travels, even how you were brought up by your grandmother when your father deserted you and then your mother remarried; but when the conversation got around to the present tense, you found something else to talk about.'

'You weren't exactly a fountain of information yourself,' she reminded him.

'I told you I was divorced and didn't believe in matrimony. What else do you want to know?'

'Not a thing——'

'Well, forgive me if I'm a little more curious. I thought about you a lot after we parted, and I couldn't help wondering why you were so cagey. I've met enough divorced women—and men—in my life to know that they're usually only too ready to talk about it. You, on the other hand, wouldn't say a thing. The only conclusion I could come up with was the obvious one—that you're still married.'

'Married!' The idea came as a complete shock to

Kathryn. 'You think that if I were married I'd . . . that I'd . . .'

'It wouldn't be the first time a woman took a little time off from marriage,' he suggested.

Kathryn felt ill. 'Did you think that all the time we were on the island?'

'Let's say I suspected it. It's the most obvious explanation, after all.'

Kathryn shook her head in disbelief. 'If that isn't just like a man. A woman has to be either married or divorced. There is another alternative, you know, and it happens to fit me. I'm single and, as strange as it may seem to you, I've always been that way.'

'Single?' The one word and the dumbfounded look on Nick's face showed that the idea had never occurred to him.

'Yes, single.'

'How did you ever manage that? I mean——'

'That I don't have a wart on the end of my nose or any obvious personality defects?' She finished for him.

He smiled sheepishly. 'Yes, well, something like that.'

Kathryn gave him a pitying look. 'It would have to be "something like that", wouldn't it? Well, I'm sorry to tell you, but as far as I know, there's no insanity in my family either. I'm just an old-fashioned Beacon Hill spinster, and how I got to be that way is none of your business. Now I've asked you to leave my house. Would you please go? I have a meal to prepare.'

But Nick didn't budge. 'I'm sorry. It doesn't wash. So maybe you're not married after all—there has to be more to it than that. A woman doesn't send a man away for no reason when she admits that she wants him as much as he wants her.'

'If that isn't the most conceited . . . I didn't admit anything of the sort——'

But he interrupted, 'Do you want me to prove it to you again?' He took a step closer.

'No! All right. You've made your point.' Kathryn
slid by him and went to the counter where the grocery
bags sat unemptied and waiting. She began to put
things away in an attempt to stall until she decided
what to tell him. An honest explanation of her
situation seemed to be the best way to get rid of him,
but her innate stubbornness made her begrudge him
any explanation at all. Married indeed!

She suddenly remembered the ice cream she'd
dropped when he had touched her, and she began to
look around on the floor. To his quizzical look she
muttered, My ice cream.'

She got down on her knees to look under the
counter, but Nick spied the container first under a
dining-room chair. 'I guess we're not the only ones
who got carried away,' he said dryly.

'Ha, ha.' Kathryn took the ice cream without
meeting his eyes.

Once the carton was safely in the freezer, she
returned to the shopping bags and got out the filet of
beef and fresh mushrooms she had purchased for Beef
Stroganoff. She unwrapped both packages and set
their contents on the cutting board next to the sink.

Nick watched her every move and finally broke into
her thoughts. 'You know, the longer you take to
answer me, the less I'll believe you. I'm already fifty
per cent sceptical of anything you might say.' He
reached across her arm, picked up a mushroom, and
popped it into his mouth. 'Are you really a caterer
who hates to cook, or was that just a good story?'

Kathryn glanced up at him and realised that he was
trying to lighten the atmosphere between them. They
had been sitting on the beach when she had told him
the improbable history of her many careers, and in
spite of herself, she smiled at the memory. 'No, that
was the truth.'

'And you were an archaeology student who hated to

dig in the dirt, a reporter who couldn't ask personal questions, a nursery school teacher who——'

'Yes, yes, and yes.' She put up a hand to still his flow of words. 'But now I'm a caterer, and however I got to be one, I have a dinner to make.' She began to slice the meat into slivers.

'Which number meal is this?' he asked as he reached for another mushroom.

'Number three.' Kathryn slapped his hand away before he ate up all her profits. His questions were re-establishing an intimacy between them that she knew she had to avoid. He had laughed when she had told him how she had become a caterer, and his laughter had made her feel that she might be almost as delightful as he seemed to find her.

She had never liked to cook, but politeness had required that she occasionally have friends over for a meal in repayment for dinners they had cooked for her. Her first efforts had been such terrible flops that, in self-defence, she had developed, one at a time, six foolproof menus which she rotated as need arose. Because she had known so little about food, she had put unusual things together; but somehow it had worked. And somehow, she had got a reputation as a creative and unusual cook.

When her last job had fallen through, an old boyfriend of hers had asked her to cater a meal for him. She'd only agreed because she'd been curious to see his new girlfriend. She had never intended to go into the catering business.

She'd made the meal, but she'd never got to see the girl. What she *had* got out of the experience was more customers. And now she had a flourishing part-time business that kept her as busy as she wanted to be and supplemented the income she received from the inheritance she'd been left by her grandmother. Like most of her careers, she hadn't chosen it as much as it had chosen her; but she liked being her own boss.

She looked up at Nick and saw that his face wore the same amused, incredulous expression it had worn when she'd first told him the tale of her sorry work history. Their eyes locked for a moment, and she decided to take advantage of his good humour to ask him to go away. He couldn't really want to ruin her whole life for the sake of a quick visit to town.

She sliced a piece of the red meat and pushed it on to the growing pile. 'Look,' she said, 'I don't think I owe you anything, but if I *do* tell you the truth, will you promise to go—and stay away?'

'If you can convince me that it's what you really want.' He leaned against the refrigerator and put his hands in his pockets. His expression remained sceptical, but since she planned to tell the truth, she didn't take him up on it. If she threw him out, there was always the chance he might return. If she persuaded him to go, he'd be more likely to stay away.

'It's quite simple,' she said, still slicing away at the meat, 'I'm not married, but I *am* engaged and I plan to *be* married very soon. What happened at the beach was a big mistake and something I never planned. I'm not proud of what I did, and I don't intend to let it happen again—ever.'

'Not even with your husband-to-be?'

'I'm planning a marriage, not an affair.'

'Are the two mutually exclusive then?'

Kathryn took her eyes off her knife and almost sliced a finger. 'Look. You wanted the truth and there it is. I don't need your sarcastic remarks.'

'Let me get this straight.' Nick stood away from the refrigerator and came to lean over her shoulder, making it no easier to do her job. 'It's OK to be unfaithful to a fiancé but not to a husband. Is that the distinction?'

'I wasn't engaged to him then.'

'But your time with *me* convinced you that you should marry *him*?'

Kathryn swung around, using her knife as a pointer. 'Listen. You'll never know the sleepless nights I spent being sorry I ever met you. I went out to that island to decide about getting married. After what happened between us, I came home convinced that I shouldn't marry *anyone*.'

'But in one short month you changed your mind?'

'I had it changed for me. Some men are big enough to take a person the way she is.'

'You told your boyfriend about us?'

'My *fiancé*,' Kathryn corrected. 'And yes, of *course* I told him—not your name or all the sordid details, but enough. *He* thought it was probably a good idea that I'd got that sort of thing out of my system.'

'Out of your system! You make it sound like the measles.'

'I wish I'd *had* the measles. At least they wouldn't have come back. I am getting married next month, and I plan to forget I ever met you. Understand?'

'And your *fiancé* will have something to hold over your head for as long as you live. It sounds like he's got you right where he wants you.'

'Northrop isn't like that.'

'*Northrop?*'

'It's an old family name.'

'Doesn't he have a nickname?'

'He doesn't need one. His name suits *him* and *he* suits *me*. Do I make myself clear?'

Without realising it, she had pointed her knife at Nick's stomach. He deflected her arm and made a placating gesture. 'You've made your point. No need to get violent. In fact I wish you luck. If you're planning to get married, you're going to need it.'

'There's no "if" about it,' Kathryn assured him.

'Then I guess I should offer you my congratulations.' He put out his hand to shake hers, but Kathryn was smarter than to take it. He chuckled and put his hand back in his pocket.

Then he looked up at the ceiling and said in a nonchalant tone, 'Maybe I'll see you both around town. Did I mention that I was moving the head office of my consulting firm to the Boston area?'

Kathryn waited for the punch line, but none was forthcoming. 'Is that some kind of joke?'

'What do you mean, joke?'

'You said you worked from San José and only came to New England to visit the area you grew up in.'

He shrugged. 'I didn't think you'd be interested.'

'Not interested! When you were going to be living in my back yard?' She couldn't afford to have this man within one hundred miles of her.

'We didn't exactly exchange addresses——'

'You knew I lived in Boston!'

'But I didn't plan to look you up—I mean . . .' He had the grace to flush. 'I mean we . . . I . . . how was I supposed to know how much I'd miss you?' He looked at her hair, her face, her breasts.

Kathryn could think of no suitable reply. His look was melting her insides, but if she gave into impulse, everything would be ruined. He had no right to arrive on her doorstep and make her feel this way.

She steeled herself against him and began, 'You can't . . . I won't let you . . .'

He laughed at the expression on her face. 'Don't look so worried. I won't say a word to Norwood when we meet.'

'Northrop,' Kathryn corrected automatically. She hadn't even been thinking of him. She realised that she was gripping the knife so tightly that her fingers had begun to cramp. She placed it on the counter as though it might break and said carefully, 'I don't care if you move down the street. There can be nothing between us, and you have no right to harass me. If you do, I shall call the police, do you understand?'

'You don't mean that.' Nick began to move in on her again.

But by now Kathryn had herself well in hand. She didn't back away but walked deliberately across the room and opened the door. 'Goodbye, Nick. You should never have come here. The kind of affair you're interested in no longer interests me. I don't want to see you again—ever!'

Nick sauntered across the room at a maddeningly slow pace and picked up her bra from where he'd flung it when he'd begun to make love to her. He folded it in his hands and it was as though he were touching her again. Then he smiled lazily and handed it to her as he passed. 'You'd better put this on. You look much too fetching bouncing around the room like that. It's a sight I shall take away and cherish in my dreams.' He walked out and didn't look back.

For a moment Kathryn was too stunned by his crudeness to move. Then she slammed the door behind him and threw her offending undergarment across the room. 'You rotten, unspeakable cad. You . . . you Russian!' She folded her arms over her breasts in a belatedly protective gesture, and listened as he ran lightly down the wooden stairs.

She felt like running to the window to scream at him as he left the building, but her upbringing wouldn't allow it. Still, she crossed to the window if only to throw a murderous look at him as he walked away.

But he didn't appear, and after a few seconds went by, she realised what must have happened. He'd been waylaid by Julia Quimby. Even as Kathryn watched, he was probably being lured into the elderly lady's flat to be offered a cup of tea.

'Ha! It serves him right,' she muttered.

But on the heels of that thought came the realisation that he might tell Julia more than she ought to know. Kathryn was halfway to the door on her way to break up their little *tête-à-tête* when she heard voices in the hall and then the outside door opened and closed.

She fled to the window just in time to see Nick turn in the street to look up at her. She backed away, but not before he'd seen her and given her a mock salute When she risked another look, he was gone.

Oh, how did I ever let such a man get close to me? she wondered. He was . . . he was . . . *all man?*

'No!' she said aloud. She couldn't have it. He was impossible and she hoped he was gone for good. Especially now that Julia had taken an interest in him.

Kathryn loved her old tenant—who was her last link to her grandmother, whom she missed terribly—but Julia did not approve of Kathryn's plan to marry Northrop, and she made her opinions very plain. The last thing Kathryn needed was to have Julia learn about the affair with Nick. It might ruin everything.

Twice before in her life Kathryn had almost married, but something had interfered each time. She'd always assumed that there would be other chances, but now time was running out. In her darkest moments, she feared that she might be fickle and unsteady like her father, and the thought was intolerable.

Such ideas had never entered her head while her grandmother was alive, because her grandmother had given her more love than anyone deserved. But Helen Gardner had been gone for two years now, and she'd left a huge empty space in Kathryn's heart.

In a way Northrop was a replacement for her grandmother, and Kathryn knew it. He was steady and dependable and wanted a family as much as she did. They needed each other and would build a good—if not exciting—life together. She couldn't afford to let anything go wrong.

She sighed and went back to the counter to finish cutting up the meat and mushrooms for the Stroganoff. She'd have to warn Julia not to encourage Nick, but she had no time to do it now.

She glanced at the clock and suddenly remembered, 'Good grief, my rice!' It was too late now for brown rice; she'd have to make white. She got out a pan, filled it with water, and shook her head in wonder that she ever managed to get a meal together at all.

CHAPTER TWO

By seven o'clock everything was ready and packed in inexpensive throwaway containers. Kathryn had worked out a system in which she cooked the meal, delivered it, and then left it for her customer to serve. She suspected that some of her customers passed the dinners off as their own creations, but that didn't bother her. Her concern ended as soon as she delivered the food and collected her cheque. If she had had such a service available when she had first developed her six foolproof meals, she might never have learned to cook at all.

She put the food in her carryall and placed it by the door while she went up to her bedroom to change her clothes. As she slipped on a new bra, she tried not to think of how the other one had come off. Nick had no right to come back into her life to reinfect her with a longing for him. His intentions were purely dishonourable and he made no secret of it.

The telephone rang just as Kathryn was about to go out of the door. She considered ignoring it in case it was Nick. But she knew that it might be a customer. Not for the first time, she wished she had an answering service.

She reached it on the fourth ring. 'Hello?'

'Kathryn, my dear, I was beginning to think you weren't home.'

'Oh, Northrop.' Kathryn put down her carryall as she recognised the rather nasal tones of her fiancé. Somehow his Boston accent seemed more pronounced than usual. Her own accent had been drilled out of her by years of diction lessons her grandmother had insisted upon. 'I was just going out to deliver a meal, but I have a few minutes,' she said brightly.

'Then that's all I'll take,' Northrop replied. 'I'm afraid something's come up here at the bank and I won't be able to see you this evening. I hope you aren't too disappointed.'

'Oh no, of course not. I mean I'll miss you, but I understand.' Kathryn realised that she had almost forgotten that he was coming.

'I knew you would. You never give me a hard time and I appreciate it. Let me tell you, I am happy to be marrying such a sensible woman.'

'Why . . . um . . . thank you. I try to be,' Kathryn was a little flustered by his praise. No one in her whole life had ever considered her sensible, except Northrop, and she still found it disconcerting.

'Well, I won't keep you. I have some people waiting for me and I know you have your delivery. Good night, my dear.'

'Good night.' Kathryn heard the line go dead, and she replaced her own receiver.

She sighed and made a face at herself. She wished that Northrop's opinion of her didn't make her feel so uncomfortable. She certainly planned to be sensible for the rest of her life, but she knew she hadn't done a good job of it so far. Her history—especially when it came to men—had been more spontaneous than wise.

The last time she'd been in love was five years ago in Paris, and it had been a whirlwind sort of thing. Paul Danton had been in the process of getting a divorce, and he'd asked her to marry him as soon as he was free.

But her grandmother had become gravely ill at the time, and she'd had to come home. Although Paul had asked her to wait for him, he had not waited for her. Their love affair had not survived the separation.

Kathryn had never been sorry that she'd come home

to be with her grandmother. She'd told herself that it had been all for the best. But still, in the end, she'd been left alone. It had been a terrible time. She'd thought that there were no dependable men left in the world.

But then she had met Northrop.

And now, all her doubts were about herself. Was she dependable enough for him? *I will be. I must be. I'll make myself be!*

A picture of Nick's grinning face flashed across her mind, but she banished it immediately. No more fly-by-night lovers for her. If he came back, she'd send him off so fast his head would spin.

And on that positive thought, she picked up her carryall and went about the business of delivering her meal.

Her old black Mercedes, a legacy from her grandmother like everything else she owned, was parked in its usual spot by the corner; and she got in and put the food next to her on the seat. She started the engine and then gave all her attention to driving through the heavy evening traffic of Boston's winding streets.

It was almost an hour later before she returned to Beacon Hill and she remembered that she had planned to stop by and see Julia Quimby. She wished she could forget all about Nick Varganin's visit that afternoon, but it was important to tell Julia that Nick was not a welcome visitor in their house. The last thing Kathryn needed was to have Julia encourage the man.

But as it turned out, she didn't get a chance to tell Julia anything. When she drove on to her street, she saw a silver-grey Porsche parked by the corner, in *her* parking spot, and she recognised it at once as Nick's. Her heart sank even as her anger rose at his nerve in coming back.

'How dare he!' She didn't know if she meant his coming back or taking her parking space.

She had to park several blocks up the street—as he must have earlier, or she would have seen his car—and she thought up half-a-dozen choice things she could say to him—after she enlightened him about the sanctity of parking spaces. She'd made it very clear that she never wanted to see him again.

Her anger grew with every step that she took back down the hill, and by the time she turned on to her front path, she was breathing fire.

Then the front door opened and out came Julia Quimby clinging to Nick's arm and looking for all the world like some elderly Cinderella in an old-fashioned pink satin dress and a full-length mink coat.

Julia beamed when she saw Kathryn. 'Oh, my dear, I'm so glad you're home. Nick is taking me out to dinner because he insists that you and I are the only people he knws in Boston, but I wish you'd come with us—unless you are seeing Northrop, that is.' She made it sound as though 'seeing Northrop' were something like going to the dentist.

Kathryn stood rooted to the spot. She wanted to throttle Nick, but she held on to her temper. The sight of him dressed in a grey business suit like a wolf in sheep's clothing, standing next to Julia in her mink and satin, was so ludicrous, and yet she was so angry that she didn't know whether to laugh or to spit.

'Hello, Julia, Nick,' she managed to get out. 'I . . . um . . . I didn't expect to see you so soon again, Nick.' She smiled with her lips, but her eyes sent Nick a murderous message.

'I just couldn't stay away from you lovely ladies,' Nick answered, ignoring her silent message.

'May I ask where you're going?'

'We have reservations at the Ritz,' Nick said urbanely. 'Both you and Norton are welcome to join us if you'd like.'

'*Northrop* is busy tonight, and I'm afraid that I've suddenly got a terrible headache,' Kathryn replied, giving him a speaking look.

'Then we mustn't keep you talking,' Julia broke in. 'You go right upstairs and take some aspirin and you'll be fine in no time.' She took Nick's arm again, and he escorted her down the steps.

Kathryn stood aside and racked her brain for some way to stop them, but she could think of nothing she could do that wouldn't look strange.

As they passed her, she got a strong whiff of Julia's perfume, and she had to stifle a gasp. The lady must have used half a bottle of Chanel No 5. Kathryn's eyes met Nick's over Julia's head, and this time it was her turn to smile.

'I hope you have a wonderful time,' she said sweetly.

'Oh, we will, won't we, Julia?' Nick patted his elderly date's arm. 'We plan to have a high old time talking about the good old days in Boston. It's been a long time since I went to school here.'

Kathryn felt an immediate sense of panic. He couldn't really mean to stick to the silly story he'd made up about their going to school together. The idea was crazy. He didn't know anything about Boston or her school years.

She caught his arm as he opened the car door. She directed her words at Julia, but her eyes pleaded with him. 'Please don't bore Nick talking about me all evening, Julia. I'm sure there are better things to discuss.'

Nick's widening grin told her that he had got the message, but his next words didn't help at all. 'Why, Katie, you sound as though you have something to hide. Have you been up to interesting things since school? I never would have thought it of you.'

'Humph,' Julia snorted. 'She's about as interesting

as a Red Sox game. Now her grandmother and I, *we* had some good times together.' She lowered herself carefully into the low-slung car and Nick shut the door.

The draught from the closing door sent another strong whiff of perfume in Kathryn's direction and she wrinkled her nose and gave Nick an evil smile. 'I hope you get held up in a traffic jam and your windows stick shut.'

Nick laughed lightly and parried, 'Don't give me another thought; and don't, for goodness sake, worry about what we might be saying. I'd hate to think of you spending the whole evening worrying about your reputation—especially with that headache.' His hand came up for a quick caress of her cheek, and then he ducked around and got into the car.

Kathryn's eyes threw darts of fire at his back, but she managed to smile and wave at the two of them as they pulled away from the kerb. Inside she was thinking, 'I'll get you for this, Nick Varganin.'

She spent a miserable evening trying not to think about Nick and what he might be saying to Julia Quimby. She changed into some old clothes, vacuumed her flat, did a load of laundry, and took a shower and washed her hair; but nothing she did took her mind off Nick for long. He had the power to ruin all her plans, and he seemed to think it was a joke.

It was one thing for Northrop to forgive her for an indiscretion with a man they'd never see again, but it was quite another for the man to arrive in town and flaunt his connection with her. It was bad enough that she couldn't stop remembering what had happened between them.

Just the sight of his grey Porsche had sent her memory flying back to Block Island and one evening when they'd driven out to a deserted beach to watch the sunset. After the sun had gone down and it had got dark, Nick had pulled her out of the car and into the minuscule shelf of a back seat. There had been barely enough room to breathe, but he had begun to make love to her like some teenage Casanova.

She'd kept saying, 'No, Nick. Oh no. Not here. No!' But he had, and they had, and afterwards she had not been able to find her tennis shoes. The next morning Nick had found them and hung them over his rear-view mirror as a trophy from the night before.

Their whole time on the island had been like something out of a dream; and after she'd come home, she'd tried to tell herself that it *had* been a dream— and something never to be repeated. Northrop had forgiven her and she had to put it all behind her.

It was ten o'clock and Kathyrn was pacing the floor when she heard Nick and Julia come in. She had no thought of going to the door until she actually found herself there; and then it took all her willpower not to open the door and call down to them. She had to know what they'd said!

Her hand was frozen to the doorknob when she heard Julia say, 'Why don't you go up and see how Kathryn is? I'm sure she's not asleep yet. Her lights are on.'

'Good idea. She'll probably want to know that I brought you home safely,' came Nick's answer, and then his footsteps sounded on the stairs.

Kathryn bolted away from the door as though it had suddenly grown hot. Her hands flew to her hair, and she looked down at her loose cotton drawstring trousers and flapping man's shirt. It was her typical 'at home' outfit, but it was not exactly becoming. She was halfway up the stairs to her room with some incoherent thought of changing when Nick rapped lightly on her door.

She stopped on the stairs and considered not answering or telling him to go away, but she realised that she was acting like an idiot. What possible difference did it make how she looked?

She called out, 'Who is it?' as though she didn't know very well, and his answer came, 'It isn't Little Red Riding Hood.'

His words brought back such a rush of memories that Kathryn found herself growing warm all over. It was a joke he'd used on her at the beach cottage when he planned to be at his worst as the Big Bad Wolf. It was totally unfair of him to use it now. If Julia were listening, it would sound completely innocent, but innocence had nothing at all to do with the feelings he aroused in her.

'Very funny,' she muttered as she reluctantly walked back down the stairs and opened her door to find him leaning against the hall wall.

His eyes took in her loose, unflattering clothing, and he grinned mockingly. 'Expecting company?'

Kathryn pushed a wisp of just-washed hair out of her eyes and glared at him. 'Did you come up here to insult me or just to give me a hard time?'

'*Julia* suggested I come see if your headache is any better,' he said loudly and then aimed a small wave towards the bottom of the stairs.

Kathryn stuck her head out the door and followed suit as he finished *sotto voce*, 'I thought you might be interested in hearing how our evening went.'

Kathryn was dying of curiosity and Nick knew it. She wanted to give him a few choice words, but she couldn't with Julia standing down there listening to them. Instead, she called down to her neighbour, 'I'm much better now, thank you. Did you have a good time?'

'Oh yes, my dear. I only wish you could have joined us. Nick is such good company. But now I have to get my old bones to bed. You'll see Nick out, won't you, dear?' She gave another small wave and retired to her flat.

Her sweet old lady act was a sham, but Kathryn made no comment other than to shake her head resignedly. What, after all, could she say?

Nick walked in through the door, and Kathryn resisted the impulse to throw him out. There was no point in making a scene now, and she *was* curious to know how the evening had gone.

As he passed her she got a strong whiff of Chanel No. 5 and she wrinkled her nose and sniffed significantly, 'Phew!'

Nick laughed and made airing motions with his jacket. 'I'll have to get this suit cleaned, but it was worth it all to find out that you had blonde hair when you were a baby, and that you were so skinny they called you "Beanpole" at that fancy academy you attended.' He looked her up and down and added, 'You haven't changed much at that.'

Kathyrn ignored his personal remark. If she had ever longed for a sexier frame, he'd be the last to know it. 'The name was "String Bean" not "Beanpole",' she corrected him. 'You must have had a fascinating evening. Did she happen to mention what years I got my wisdom teeth?'

'I'd say they haven't done you much good,' Nick grinned. 'Now aren't you the least bit interested in what *I* told *her*?'

Kathryn knew that she had been bandying words with him to avoid just that subject. She was afraid of what he might say. She swallowed and gave him an unconsciously appealing look. 'You didn't give me away, did you?'

'Now would I do that?' He came towards her and reached out to put an arm around her shoulders.

But Kathryn backed away. 'I don't know what you'd do. That's why I'm asking.'

He stopped pursuing her and seemed to consider for a moment. Then his blue eyes gleamed roguishly. 'What will you give me to find out?'

'About five seconds,' she replied coldly. She told herself that the thrill that went up her spine at his suggestive tone was anger. 'If you're going to bait me, you can leave now.'

She began to stalk towards the door, but it was a mistake. His arm snaked out and grabbed her, and he brought her stormy brown eyes to within inches of his laughing blue ones. 'Don't be so prickly,' he chided her. 'I didn't tell Julia anything, I let her tell me all about you and then, when I knew enough about your swanky academy, I told her that I had got a scholarship to attend for my last two years and that's how I met you. She doesn't suspect a thing. Now don't you think you owe me a show of appreciation for my cleverness?'

Kathryn had begun to relax as she listened, but his hands began to massage her arms and his eyes were drinking in the line of her throat and the open neck of her shirt.

'I don't owe you anything,' she said, trying to slip out of his grasp. 'I told you to go away and stay out of my life and I meant it. You had no right to talk to Julia.'

'No right?' He let her go and grinned as she buttoned her shirt to her neck. 'What's the matter, were you jealous?'

'You're very funny, Nick. You know why I don't want you around. What I don't understand is why *you* want to make trouble for *me*. What did I ever do to you?'

'What did you do to me? You really want to know?' Nick let go of her and threw his hands up in the air. 'You got under my skin, that's what you did. You made me want you. I couldn't get you out of my mind once I'd left the island. I found myself looking you up in the phone book the minute I got to Boston, though I had firmly decided not to. I thought you might be married but I didn't care. And now that I'm here, the least you can do is let me hold you.' He reached out to her.

But she backed away. 'Wait a minute. You make it sound like some kind of deal I welshed on. Is my memory faulty, wasn't it you who declared that he didn't believe in long-term arrangements? Don't tell me you've changed your mind.'

'Didn't you hear me, Katie? I told you I want you and what's more I know you want me, isn't that enough?' He'd backed her to the wall beside the door and now he put his hands on either side of her head. Kathryn felt trapped and not a little frightened by her own response to his nearness, but she was determined not to let Nick see how strongly he affected her.

'No, it isn't enough. Didn't *you* hear what I told you this afternoon? Wanting is for babies and people with no plans for the future. I'm tired of men like you who kiss and run.'

But her words did no good. He just smiled and taunted her, 'I'm not the one who's running now, am I?' He bent his head towards hers.

Kathryn began to twist her head aside, but then she thought better of it. She'd show him how little he meant to her. She let his mouth cover hers but kept her own lips tightly shut and unresponsive.

She thought he'd give up as soon as he realised that he was getting nowhere with her, but she under-estimated her man. Once he saw that she intended to remain as stiff as a block of wood, he gave her a mocking smile and said, 'OK, Katie, if that's the way you want it——'

He took one hand away from the wall and began to unbutton her shirt. His eyes dared her to let him.

Kathryn swallowed and tried to decide what to do. He had turned her little lesson into a game and she hated to be a loser; but how far could she afford to let him go? There was nothing but bare skin underneath her baggy shirt and drawstring trousers, and her breasts were already exposed to his view.

He finished unbuttoning her shirt and then began to stroke the side of her breast with the back of his hand. His smile had disappeared, and there was only desire on his face. 'Tell me if this hurts, will you?'

Kathryn shut her eyes. His touch reminded her that he knew every sensitive part of her body, and he wasn't above exploring each one of them if she didn't stop him. He had no scruples at all—something she should have remembered before she'd started their little duel.

'OK, Nick, you win——' she began, but she didn't get to finish. As soon as she opened her mouth, he took the opportunity to cover it with his own. He pulled her away from the wall and against his body where the evidence of his arousal was only too evident. His hands cupped her buttocks and made her feel his need of her.

She tried to push against him, but she had let things go too far. Inside her head her voice was crying, *Stop him, you fool. He'll ruin everything for you.* But the roaring of her blood drowned it out.

Her resistance could only be called feeble when he untied the drawstring of her trousers and let them slide to the floor. He slipped out of his jacket and began unbuttoning his own shirt as he released her lips and lowered her on to the thick carpeting. His eyes devoured her body and forewarned her of the places that his hands and lips would soon invade.

He made a pillow of his shirt for her head and then smiled down at her, letting her see the desire that flamed behind his eyes. 'Hello, my Katie,' he said gruffly. 'You'll never know how much I've missed this.'

He kissed her eyelids shut while his hand caressed

her gently from the sensitive side of her breast across her stomach to the smoothness of her thighs. Then his mouth claimed hers softly and insinuatingly at the same time as his hand slid between her thighs to separate them for his exploration.

His knowing lips and fingers worked together to demolish any last resistance she might have put up if he hadn't known exactly where to touch her. She tried one last time to say, 'No, no, no,' but all that came out was a sigh. He was too aware of her every secret place.

She let her thighs fall apart and brought up her hands to nestle in the thick short hair at the back of his head. Her back arched to push her breasts into the hardness of his chest. She felt herself give way completely to the need to feel skin against silken skin.

It was only the telephone, which suddenly began to ring, that stopped them from completing their union. At first they ignored it, but it went on ringing until Nick groaned deep in his throat and released her lips from his.

He raised his head and scowled at her. 'My god, woman, what is this? Do you have the place wired to ring whenever the level of passion gets too high?'

Kathryn shivered and swallowed before she could speak. 'It's the telephone. I have no control over it at all.' Nor had she any control over herself, came the despairing thought.

'Let it ring,' he said gruffly and bent to claim her lips again with his own.

But the spell was broken, and Kathryn turned her head away from his kiss. The insistency of the ringing meant that it could be only one person. A person who knew she was at home because she wasn't with him.

She was thankful for the interruption even as her body cried out in disappointment. 'I've got to answer it,' she said shakily. 'I know who it is.'

She pushed Nick away from her and reached across

the floor for her shirt. She wrapped it around her, glad of its long, concealing tails, and she trembled in disbelief at what she had almost let happen.

She got to her feet and tottered to the phone which hung on the kitchen wall. She picked up the receiver as though it might bite her and said, 'Hello.' Her voice was ragged and breathless and she hoped he wouldn't notice.

'Hello? Kathryn? Did I wake you up, my dear?'

'No . . . I mean sort of . . . I was um . . . reading and I must have dozed off.' She kept her back to Nick and tried to pretend he wasn't there.

'Well, I won't keep you from your dreams,' Northrop said heartily. 'I just called to tell you that I missed you this evening; and I wanted to remind you that tomorrow is Saturday and we're going furniture shopping. I trust you haven't forgotten?'

'No, of course not. I'm looking forward to it, darling.' She had never called Northrop darling before, and it rolled poorly off her tongue; but she felt she had to make her ties to him clear for Nick—and maybe for herself.

'Very good then.' His tenor voice sounded pleased. 'I'll come for you at ten. Good night . . . er . . . darling.'

'Good night.' Kathryn hung up the phone and wished she could sink through the floor. She felt lower than she could ever remember feeling. She was the worst sort of traitor, and she didn't want to face the man who was the cause of her disloyalty.

She pulled her shirt more tightly around her and ignored the ripping sound that meant she must have torn a seam somewhere. Then she steeled herself to turn towards Nick. 'Are you satisfied now? That was my fiancé—you know—the man I plan to marry? If you had . . . if we'd . . .'

She couldn't say it, but Nick had no trouble. 'If we'd made love, you mean?'

'You know what I meant! You could have ruined everything! Whatever you may think of me, I don't *do* this sort of thing. I *won't* do it. Northrop may have forgiven me once, but I haven't really forgiven myself. You got to me tonight because I wasn't ready for you. But I'm ready now, and it won't happen again.'

Nick listened to her with a faint, almost amused, smile upon his face. He pointed to her shirt and seemed to want to tell her something, but she gave him no chance to break in.

By the time she had finished, he seemed to change his mind. He gave her a sceptical look and said, 'All you had to do was send me away. I wouldn't say you tried so very hard.'

'I don't care what you'd say, I'm trying now, and I mean it. Go away and please stay out of my life. I want to forget I ever met you.'

'Is that why you're marrying Norwood, so you can forget me? Does he make you feel the way I do?'

'Northrop,' Kathryn corrected wearily. She did not even grow warm in Northrop's arms, and she sensed that Nick knew it.

She looked at him and passed a hand over her eyes. 'The only thing I feel right now is rotten, Nick. All you want to do is spoil things for me. You don't play fair.'

'Play fair?' Nick looked at her and seemed to have a hard time taking his eyes off her shirt. His lips tried to smile, but he held them immobile. 'You don't exactly play fair yourself, my dear. I'll give you the benefit of the doubt and assume that you don't know how tempting you look standing there, but you expect too much of a man.'

'Oh no, I don't. All I want you to do is go. And I don't expect you to come back. That's easy enough to understand, isn't it?'

He nodded and seemed about to say something

more, but then he shook his head and went to the door. As he opened it, he gave her one last look, raised his eyebrows mockingly, and then was gone. His footsteps on the stairs made a final punctuation to his departure.

Kathryn let out a long quavering sigh as the door shut. For a moment she'd been afraid that he might try to make love to her again, and she wasn't at all sure she was up to fighting him. Her wayward body seemed to want to try its best to ruin her careful plans.

She let the shirt she had been clutching around her hang loose and then noticed that the tearing sound she had heard had been the armhole seam. It was a large tear and she suddenly had a horrible thought. She wrapped the shirt around her again and went over to look in the mirror by the door.

What she saw made her groan in dismay as she realised why Nick had shown such an interest in her shirt. It had not been the shirt he'd been staring at but her breast which protruded more than halfway through the opening. She must have been standing like that the whole time they had been talking. No wonder he had called her a temptress.

She wanted to run after him and tell him that she had not known about the tear, but he was long gone and she didn't really want to face him again—with or without her clothes on. Whether or not he believed her, her embarrassment would be the same.

'Oh, Kathryn, can't you ever do anything right?' she said disgustedly as she rewrapped the shirt in a less revealing manner and climbed wearily up the stairs to her bedroom. Was she destined to do something stupid every time she saw him?

She gave another long sigh and then caught herself up on that last thought. There'd be no problem with doing stupid things because she was not going to see him anymore. He'd never even get close to her again, she'd make sure of that.

She crawled tiredly under the soft duvet on her bed without bothering to wash her face or brush her teeth or take off her torn shirt. She curled up in a ball and hugged her knees to her chest and let the shudder of unfulfilled passion run through her until she could relax.

'One thing's for sure, Kathryn', she muttered to herself. 'Now you know why you did what you did on that island. That man is poison to you.'

When she'd come back from holiday she hadn't been able to understand why she'd let herself have an affair with Nick when it might have ruined everything for her. But now she understood only too well. Nick Varganin had the power to make her want him—physically at least—no matter what her common sense told her. Most men stopped when you said, 'No.' Nick took it as a cue to be more physically persuasive.

And could she blame him? 'No' was a weak word when you were melting in a man's arms. What was there about him that made her forget her own name?

'I won't have it, Nick, I won't,' she said into the depths of her pillow. 'I know what I want and it isn't you!'

She fell asleep with the pillow over her head, swearing to forget him; but her unconscious mind, like her body, was not through with him yet.

CHAPTER THREE

THE dream she'd been having since she'd returned from her holiday came again in all its force. It was a replay of her whole time with Nick on the island with the added vividness of her imagination to make it even worse.

They'd met on the ferry going over. Nick's car had been parked behind hers in the bow of the boat, and they'd smiled at each other in the impersonal manner of strangers as they'd inched their way out of their car doors, trying not to scratch the paint on the car next to them. Nick had a much harder time getting his large torso out into the narrow space between vehicles.

'They pack us in like sardines,' he said with a grin as he squeezed his body out. Kathryn smiled sympathetically at his difficulty, and then stood with him for a few minutes while they waited for the way to clear to the stairs.

They watched the bowels of the boat fill up with every description of car and van, and soon the fumes from the exhausts began to bother Kathryn. She made a waving motion in the air. 'This is worse than the city.'

Nick made a face and agreed. 'Yes, let's get out of here. I'm heading for a seat on the upper deck.'

He led Kathryn between cars to the metal staircase and then allowed her to go up in front of him. They reached the main deck together and were caught in the onrush of passengers who had not brought cars.

'I don't think there'll be any room to sit down,' Kathryn called to him above the noise.

'Then we'd better be quick.' Nick grabbed her hand

and pulled her behind him until they arrived, gasping for air, on the top deck. Given a choice, Kathryn would have gone her own way, but he didn't ask.

The seats were filling up fast, but he found two together almost at the prow of the boat. He pulled her down with him, again without asking, and gave her a satisfied smile. 'There, we just made it.'

Kathryn was too breathless to object. His friendliness was unexpected and more than she would have sought, but she appreciated having a seat. She gave him another impersonal, stranger-to-stranger smile, hoping he'd sense that she wasn't looking for a man, but he didn't seem to notice.

He put out his hand. 'I'm Nick Varganin, by the way.'

Kathryn's hand went out automatically and was swallowed in the largeness of his. She liked the size and feel of his grip in spite of herself. He seemed so safe and friendly and not at all threatening. It showed how appearances could deceive.

Her smile warmed a bit and she said simply, 'I'm Kathryn Lawrence.'

'Pleased to meet you, Kathryn.' He didn't start calling her Katie until much later. 'Are you going out to visit friends?' His question seemed casual, and Kathryn answered it the same way.

'No, I've rented a cottage by myself.' She'd chosen Block Island because no one she knew ever went there.

'I've got a place by myself, too,' he said. His smile changed a bit, and he gave her an assessing look.

Kathryn realised later that she should have been warned by that look, but she read nothing in his smile. They enjoyed the rest of the ferry ride, and when the boat arrived at the island, they parted company with nothing said about future meetings.

When they ran into each other the next morning on the beach it was a complete coincidence. 'Hi. We must be neighbours,' he greeted her. 'Do you mind if I walk along with you?'

'No, of course not.' It seemed like such an innocent thing to do.

The beach stretched out in front of them until it came to an abrupt end in the distance at an ungainly pile of boulders that looked as though they'd been tumbled by some giant hand. Nick fell into step beside her, and they left two sets of prints in the hard cold sand at the water's edge.

Nick's prints were large and deep and Kathryn's small, narrow and much more shallow. As they walked along, she couldn't resist saying, 'You make a big impression.'

He laughed and said, 'I guess I have to do it somehow. You didn't seem to be too impressed on the boat.'

'I don't usually talk to strangers.' It came out more coolly than she'd intended.

'Ah yes, I had the feeling I was intruding.' He put his hands in the pockets of his rolled-up slacks and kicked at a pile of seaweed that had been washed up on the beach.

Kathryn glanced sideways at him and saw that his smile was wry. 'I came out here to be alone,' she explained.

At that he stopped in his tracks and looked down at her, blocking the sun with his tall frame. 'Then I guess I should be walking the other way.' He turned as if to go.

Kathryn immediately felt contrite. She was being unforgivably rude to this man who was only a friendly neighbour, after all. 'No. I'm sorry.' She put a hand on his arm. 'I didn't mean that the way it sounded. You have every right to walk this way.'

'I guess I could always follow ten paces behind, and we can pretend we never met,' he suggested.

Kathryn winced. 'You could, but I wish you wouldn't.' The silliness of the situation made them both smile, and they resumed their walk in a more companionable atmosphere.

Kathryn was immensely attracted to him even then, but she didn't admit it to herself until days later. He invited her to have lunch with him and she accepted. She felt so *comfortable* with him.

Over the next few days, their relationship built gradually. They talked about everything but themselves. At one point Nick mentioned that he was divorced, but Kathryn quickly changed the subject. She found that she didn't want to tell him about Northrop, even though she knew that she should.

She didn't stop to examine the motives behind her silence. If she had, she might have prevented what followed.

It took Nick four days to get her into his bed, and by then it seemed like the natural culmination of what had begun on the ferry. She was no longer the same Kathryn Lawrence who had got on the boat. Nick had turned her into his Katie; and by the time he made his move, she was more than ready for him—he was so big, so gentle, so *knowing*.

That day they had taken their usual morning constitutional on the beach, and they'd picnicked later on the rocks. Kathryn had gone back to her cottage to shower and rest in the afternoon, and then she'd gone over to his place where he was cooking their dinner. He was not a bad cook for a man.

After dinner they sat on the old-fashioned swing on his front porch. They'd sat on the same swing for three nights running because his porch was screened against mosquitoes, but this time it was different. There was an electricity between them, and when he put his arm around her, it felt like coming home.

'I love this time of evening,' he said casually, as

though this were not the first time he'd touched her in more than a perfunctory manner.

'Yes, the sky is beautiful.' Kathryn tried to match his nonchalance, even though her heart had begun to beat a mile a minute.

They sat in silence, watching the moon rise over the water. Nick's hand began to stroke her arm, and she let her head rest on his shoulder.

His first kisses were tentative and exploratory, but they soon deepened and he groaned, 'Ah, Katie, I want to make love to you.'

Alarm bells should have gone off in Kathryn's head, but she was under the spell of the island—and the spell of Nick. When he lifted her in his arms and carried her inside, she made no attempt to stop him. It had all happened so gradually, so naturally, she wasn't sure she could ever have prevented it.

She did have second thoughts, though. The next morning, when she awoke in Nick's bed, she was more than a little shocked at what they'd done. She tried to slip away, but he caught her and made love to her again—and again—until she had no more ideas of running away.

From then on, they might as well have saved the rent on one of the cottages, because they spent all their time together. They swam and picnicked, sunbathed and made love like two honeymooners who could not get enough of each other.

Kathryn sensed that what they had would not last beyond their holiday, but she couldn't seem to care. She'd come to the island to make a decision, and the decision had made itself. She couldn't marry Northrop now. She wasn't sure she'd ever really meant to.

Oh Nick, Nick, Nick. Their days together washed into a beautiful feeling of completeness; and then, as always, Kathryn awoke from her dream to find herself alone and indescribably lonely in her bed.

She blinked awake, and when her sadness had lessened somewhat, she made herself remember the rest of the story. Nick's holiday had ended a few days before hers, and he'd left the island with no mention of ever seeing her again. It was what she'd expected, but still, it had hurt. She'd spent her last two days walking the beaches alone—no Nick, and because of him, no Northrop to go home to either.

It was only when she got back to Boston that she changed her mind—or had it changed for her. Northrop had been more tolerant than any woman had a right to expect.

'What happened to you on that island is very typical, my dear. It even has a name. Wild oats, I believe it's called. I might have recommended it myself, if I had thought of it. It's best to get that sort of thing out of one's system *before* the marriage rather than *after*, wouldn't you say?'

'Yes. No. I don't know!' Kathryn said aloud in the darkness. The words 'wild oats' replayed across her mind like a broken record. It *had* been wild oats, hadn't it?

She looked up at the ceiling which reflected dimly the lights from the street below and remembered that Nick had come back. Unless it had been part of her dream, he'd returned to plague her again with all her doubts.

No! I won't have it. If he ever tries to touch me again, I'll scream!

For her peace of mind, she was going to have to try to forget this day just as she'd tried to forget the island. In the morning she was going shopping with Northrop. That was reality.

She put Nick out of her mind completely and made herself think of Northrop—dependable, down-to-earth Northrop. Eventually, she fell back to sleep.

*

The next morning Northrop was on time, as always. He used the key she had given him for the outside entrance to the house and then knocked politely on the door of her flat. Julia Quimby did not stick her head out of her door as she often did with Kathryn's other friends, but Northrop was not sensible to the fact he was being slighted.

Kathryn was glad that Julia had decided to boycott her fiancé. As far as she was concerned, the less Julia saw of Northrop the better.

When she opened the door, she found that she was looking upward about a foot too high to where Nick's head would have been. She quickly adjusted her gaze downward and was rewarded with the familiar and comforting sight of her fiancé.

Northrop was just her height and balding on top, and he looked as safe and sane as the morning. Kathryn smiled in pleased welcome and put out her cheek for his kiss. This was no Don Juan who would try to sweep her off her feet, but a calm, dignified man whom she would surely come to love in time—long after the Nicks of the world had passed on to newer game.

She shook off the intrusive thought of Nick and smiled more brightly at Northrop. 'Good morning . . . Come in . . . I'll just get my bag and we'll be off.'

But Northrop stood in the door looking confused and slightly embarrassed. His eyes swept over the jeans and open-necked shirt she wore and he smiled doubtfully. 'Have I come too early? I mean . . .' His hand indicated her clothing and then his own.

Kathryn realised for the first time that he was wearing a navy three-piece suit. She was so used to seeing him in a suit that she hadn't noticed, but it was the last thing she would have expected him to wear for a Saturday shopping date. 'I thought we were just going to browse along Newbury Street.' It was her turn to be doubtful.

'Um . . . well, yes. Though I hope we do more than browse. We want to refurbish our suite before the snow flies.' He gave a little laugh and continued to look uncomfortable, but his good manners seemed to forbid any more direct attack upon her outfit.

Kathryn had to suppress a smile. She was tempted to give him a hard time, but his very stuffiness was one of the qualities she found most endearing about him. It boded well for a stable future and marriage. He was no fly-by-night fad-follower.

'Actually, I would like to change—if you don't mind waiting,' she said, as though the thought were completely her own.

'You needn't on my account,' he returned gallantly, but she could see that he was relieved at the suggestion. She kissed him lightly on the cheek and ran quickly up the spiral staircase to her top-floor bedroom.

It took her only a few minutes to dig out her old but classic grey suit and pair it with a yellow silk blouse and some low, black shoes. Until she'd met Northrop, she'd had little need of such clothes, and so her selection was not great. She'd bought a few new things for her dates with him, but she needed to buy more.

She knew that it was about time her taste in clothing matured to the new status she would have as Mrs Northrop Davis III. Jeans were for teens.

She smiled at her mental rhyme, took a last look at herself in the cheval mirror by her dresser, and joined Northrop who had seated himself patiently on her sofa.

He rose as soon as she started down the stairs. 'You look very nice, my dear.' He beamed his approval. 'You know, sales people give much better service if one dresses well.'

'I'm afraid I prefer it if they ignore me until I'm ready to buy,' Kathryn said ruefully.

'That doesn't make for very good progress, though, does it?' he replied fondly. 'We have a lot of ground to cover today if we expect to have our rooms finished by the wedding.' He referred to the suite of rooms they would share in his mansion further up Beacon Hill.

'We could live in my flat for a while, you know,' Kathryn said, but without much hope.

'We've been all over that and I'd thought you finally agreed with me that if we plan to live permanently in my home, we might as well start out there and save ourselves the trouble of moving.'

'Yes, I know,' Kathryn sighed. 'And we don't want to leave your mother rattling around in that big place alone. You're right. I agreed. It's just that . . .' She saw that he was becoming impatient and she broke off. 'Never mind. I'm ready. Shall we go?'

As they began to shop, she found that Northrop had been right about salesmen. He and she were afforded immediate respect wherever they went. She didn't know whether it was because of their clothing or Northrop's dignified demeanour, but they were treated with deference the minute they entered each store.

I must, I do, appreciate this man, she told herself.

They made excellent progress during the morning in narrowing down their choices as to a style and colour-scheme that would suit them both, but as lunchtime approached, Kathryn felt that she had had about all she could take.

She sat down on a pile of carpeting as Northrop discussed the merits of natural versus synthetic fibres with a fawning salesman, and she suddenly wanted to get out of the shop and into the sunshine. 'Let's leave this for another time and drive out to Rockport for lunch,' she suggested, giving the salesman an apologetic smile as she broke into his paean to wool.

To her surprise, Northrop agreed; but when they

got out on to the street his words disappointed her.
'I'm glad you got us out of there, my dear, but you're
not serious about Rockport, are you?'

Kathryn insisted that she was. 'We can drive along
the water and stop at the first lobster shack we see,'
she said, not really hoping that they would, but giving
him room to negotiate.

They settled on eating at the best restaurant in
Gloucester, but Kathryn was pleased. Afterwards she
persuaded him to stop at her favourite crescent of a
beach so that she could take off her shoes and
stockings and wade in the ocean water that the
summer sun had warmed almost to the temperature of
the cool September air.

She asked Northrop to join her, but he preferred to
sit on the rocky ledge above the sand and watch her.
His indulgent expression made her feel like a child,
but she told herself that someday, when they had
children of their own, he'd be right down in the waves
splashing with them.

Meanwhile, she walked down to the water alone and
raised her head to breathe in the tangy salt air. Out at
sea, sailing boats dotted the horizon; and in the
distance a larger boat moved slowly in the water.

When she saw the boat, Kathryn's mind immediately
went back to the day she had met Nick, and she shut
her eyes in despair. She would *not* let him intrude on
her day with Northrop. But the memory of their
meeting kept pushing at her mind, and soon she
decided to give up the beach.

She turned and saw that Northrop was waving at
her from the ledge where she had left him sitting. She
waved back at him and began to hurry along the hard
sand above the water line.

'You should have walked with me. The water is
wonderful,' she said as she came up to where he was
sitting.

But he only smiled and replied, 'I get as much pleasure from watching you, and my feet don't get all sandy. Now shall we get back to town?'

'Yes, I'm ready,' Kathryn smiled back. She bent down and quickly wiped her feet and put in her shoes and stockings. She'd just have to stop coming to the beach until all thoughts of Nick were in the past.

The next day was Sunday, the day she usually had dinner with Northrop and his mother in their large stone house which was situated in the most exclusive section of Beacon Hill. The mansion was beautifully set off from the street by a small garden of rhododendrons and junipers. The front entrance was wide and gracious and led off on either side to exquisitely furnished rooms that Kathryn had never seen used.

Mrs Davis received her in a small parlour at the back of the house, and they ate dinner in a long dining room that swallowed the three of them like ants. There was a young Irish maid to serve them, and the conversation was stilted as always.

'It's so nice to see you, Kathryn. Northrop doesn't bring you home often enough to suit me,' Mrs Davis said as they began to eat the first course.

'Thank you, Mrs Davis—I mean Loraine,' Kathryn corrected herself before her future mother-in-law could insist. In spite of the older woman's gracious words, Kathryn felt ill at ease with her.

'Did you have a successful shopping expedition yesterday?' Loraine Davis asked.

Northrop answered for both of them, 'I'm afraid we were distracted by the beautiful weather and ended up in Rockport, but we did manage to agree on a colour-scheme, didn't we, darling?' He looked fondly at Kathryn.

'We saw some things we liked very much,' Kathryn

agreed, grateful that he didn't blame her for what she knew he considered a wasted afternoon.

'I think it was a good plan for you to look at things together,' Mrs Davis said, 'but now that you have a better idea of what is available, perhaps you might like to speak to my decorator?'

'Now that sounds like a good compromise, doesn't it, Kathryn?' Northrop asked quickly. 'That way we'll have the best of both methods and save time into the bargain.'

Kathryn had told them that she didn't want to use a decorator, but it no longer seemed important to argue. She had been the one, after all, who had insisted that they go out to the beach rather than continue shopping.

'Whatever you do will be fine with me,' she agreed, trying not to feel manipulated.

'Then it's settled. I will make an appointment for you some time next week,' Loraine concluded. Kathryn thought she looked relieved.

Their dinner consisted of several courses, and by the time it was over, Kathryn felt drained from the attempt to keep up her end of the conversation. If she hadn't been sure that things would get much better when she actually lived there, she might have doubted her decision to marry Northrop; but she knew everything would be fine once they had a child. Children always changed a house. Mrs Davis was a widow, and Kathryn sensed she was lonely. A baby would brighten up the world for all of them.

As Northrop drove her home, Kathryn was so tired she wanted to ask him if he'd mind not coming in with her. They usually spent Sunday evenings making plans, but she was not sure she was up to it this evening.

Then, as they drove around the block looking for a place to park Northrop's Lincoln, she caught sight of

Nick's Porsche parked by the corner. Before she could stop herself, she had groaned aloud.

Northrop looked at her quickly, 'Is something the matter?'

'Oh no, nothing,' Kathryn started guiltily. 'I just thought I saw a parking space, but it was a fire hydrant.'

'Yes, I saw it too,' he agreed. 'They do tend to fool one.'

Kathryn collected herself and told herself that anyone might own a silver-grey Porsche. But she didn't believe it. Nick was around, and she only hoped that he wasn't in her hallway waiting for her. She wouldn't put it past Julia Quimby to let him in.

She almost asked Northrop to drop her off in front of the house, but she couldn't think up a plausible reason to do so. He'd be sure to suspect that something was wrong.

Northrop was in all ways a gentleman and wouldn't dream of leaving a woman on the street. He was so considerate of Kathryn that he hadn't even tried to make love to her yet. She assumed that he was waiting for their wedding night which was only a few weeks away.

His lack of passion had bothered her before, but now she was relieved. She was so confused by Nick's arrival on the scene that her emotions were in a turmoil that begged only for peace.

They finally found a place to park, and it was with much trepidation that Kathryn approached the front door. But there was no one in the hallway and sounds of music and laughter came from behind Julia's door.

'A party going on?' Northrop suggested as they went up the stairs to her flat.

'Probably some of Julia's bridge-playing friends,' Kathryn answered, hoping that her discomfort was not too obvious. She threw a look of loathing at the wall from behind which the sounds were coming and preceded Northrop into her flat.

She made some coffee as she usually did, but she could not concentrate on anything Northrop was saying. Finally he asked, 'Is there something wrong, my dear?'

'I'm sorry. I'm afraid I've got a terrible headache. I thought it would go away, but it's getting worse. Would you be offended if I asked you to leave?' All Kathryn wanted was to be left alone by the whole world.

'No, of course not. You should have said something earlier. Can I get you anything before I go?'

'I think I'll just go to bed early.'

'That sounds like a good idea,' Northrop agreed. 'You haven't been yourself tonight. Just stay where you're sitting and I'll show myself out.' He bent to kiss her and then turned towards the door.

But Kathryn was not going to risk the possibility that he might run into Nick without her. She followed him down the stairs and tried to hurry him out of the door.

But they were still in the hallway when Julia Quimby's apartment door opened to emit Kathryn's white-haired neighbour followed close behind by Nick. Kathryn had no recourse but to stop and make introductions. She saw that Northrop was looking with some surprise at Julia's guest, and she tried to minimise the encounter.

'Hello, Julia, Nick,' she said, hiding her anger at seeing them as best she could. 'Northrop, you've met Julia Quimby, my neighbour, and this is Nick Varganin. And Nick, this is Northrop Davis, my fiancé.'

Nick put out his large hand and gave Northrop an unnecessarily hearty handshake. 'How do you do?' He looked Northrop over from head to toe, and Kathryn couldn't help wishing that Northrop were taller and had more hair.

'I'm sorry if we were too noisy down here,' Julia chimed in. 'I was telling Nick about Boston in the old days and playing some of my favourite records for him.'

'Yes, I'm new in town and Julia's been kind enough to show me around and try to make me feel at home.' Nick gave Kathryn a look that told her that there was another place he would like to be made to feel at home.

Kathryn ignored him as Northrop said suavely, 'You are very lucky to have Julia for your guide.' He released his fingers from Nick's grip and flexed them experimentally as though checking to see if they still worked. 'I hope you enjoy our town,' he said as he edged towards the door with Kathryn right behind him.

But Julia didn't let them go that easily. 'I told Nick that if he has any banking to do, he should call on you, Northrop,' she said brightly. 'I hope that wasn't presumptuous of me.'

At the word 'banking' Northrop stopped at the door and turned back. He gave Nick a new, more complete perusal. 'Have you any particular needs in that direction?' he enquired, looking suddenly interested.

Kathryn felt her imaginary headache becoming real. This couldn't be happening. 'I'm sure his needs are very usual,' she said quickly and then cringed as she realised that her words could have more than one meaning.

Nick caught the *double entendre* and gave her a barely perceptible wink, but Northrop was on the scent of a possible new client and had no time for double meanings. 'What business are you in, Mr Vargaris, is it?'

'Varganin,' all three of the others corrected him in unison

Julia tittered at the coincidence, Nick looked amused, but Kathryn felt even more uncomfortable if that were possible. The whole little tableau was a farce, but she wasn't laughing.

'I consult for several firms in the semi-conductor industry,' Nick answered Northrop. 'I've been working from San José, but I'm an old New England man at heart, and half of my business is in the Boston area, so I decided to move my headquarters here. I've leased space in the new Winthrop Building. Do you know it?'

Northrop obviously did. His eyes lit up and he declared, 'An excellent location. We have a branch near there.' He reached quickly into his inside jacket pocket. 'Here, take my card. If we can be of any service to you, just give me a call. I'd be happy to arrange your account myself.'

Kathryn watched the whole transaction with a feeling of inevitability. The only thing she could be thankful for was that Julia had not introduced Nick as her old school chum. Perhaps Northrop would never have to hear that story.

She put her hand on her head and smiled weakly. 'I hate to interrupt business, but I think I'll just go back up to my flat if you gentlemen don't mind. I'm afraid my headache is getting worse.' She moved towards the stairs, knowing that Northrop would be too polite to ignore her condition.

He turned reluctantly away from Nick and put his arm around her shoulders, 'I'm sorry, my dear. It was inexcusable of me to forget you. Mr Varganin and I can get together during the week. Let me see you to your door.'

'On second thoughts, maybe some fresh air will help my head. I'll walk with you to your car,' Kathryn said quickly. She had never intended to go upstairs until she was sure Northrop was safely away.

They went out together, and she breathed a sigh of relief as he drove off. He might think he would see Nick during the week, but she had other plans. Nick would not be banking with her fiancé if there was any way she could prevent it.

She walked back inside, expecting to face both Julia and Nick, but Julia had disappeared and Nick was sitting alone on the bottom stair. Kathryn glanced at Julia's door and could bet that her neighbour was on the other side of it, listening. She glared at Nick and whispered. 'What are you doing here? I told you to stay away.'

'Julia invited me to dinner. Did you expect me to hurt her feelings and refuse?' he whispered back, giving her a wounded look.

'You should have found some pressing engagement in the other side of town,' she hissed. 'I don't want you in my house. Don't you understand? People will begin to wonder what you are doing here.'

'Would it help if I wore a sign saying, "I'm here to see Julia Quimby, not Katie Lawrence"?'

'Very funny.' Kathryn didn't laugh. She was beginning to realise that there was nothing she could do to stop Nick from coming around if Julia kept inviting him. 'You're not going to go away, are you?' she asked.

'Would you really deprive the dear lady of a bit of fun just to stop the neighbours from talking?' Nick countered.

Kathryn put a hand over her eyes. He had no right to turn things around and make her feel like the guilty party. Never in the world would she want to take anything away from Julia and he knew it.

She let out her breath and put her hands on her hips. 'All right. See her if you must, but there's at least one thing you can do for me.'

'And what's that?' Nick asked, rising to his feet.

Kathryn backed away from his overpowering height. 'You can stay away from my fiancé. There are lots of other banks in town. Use one.'

He smiled lazily down at her and drawled, 'Don't worry. I will not call on your precious Norwood. Here, you can have his card.' He held out the small, white piece of cardboard.

Kathryn refrained from correcting his mispronunciation of Northrop's name. She realised by now that he only did it to annoy her. She took the proffered card with a graceless, 'Thank you,' and stepped away from the door. 'I believe that you were just leaving?'

Nick raised his eyebrows at the coldness of her tone and took a step towards her. But she backed away and warned, 'Don't you come near me.'

Nick's face lit in a grin. 'You say that a lot, but this time I'll pretend you mean it. You look like you need a good night's sleep. Go upstairs and take care of that headache.' He leaned over and kissed her lightly before she could dodge away. Then he was gone without another word.

'Argh . . .' Kathryn curled her hands into fists and sputtered incoherently as the door closed on him. But she dared not call out after him. She was a mixture of emotions, the uppermost of which was anger. It seemed that he was going to become a fixture around the place no matter what she did.

She turned and looked at Julia's door. Her elderly tenant was the key to getting rid of Nick, but Kathryn was too tired to tackle the lady tonight. She put Julia on the agenda for the first thing in the morning and climbed the stairs to her flat door.

All her plans were teetering on the brink of disaster, and she felt like a tightrope walker. One wrong move, and her life could go down the drain.

CHAPTER FOUR

IT turned out to be two days later before she talked to Julia. When she went downstairs the next morning, Julia had already gone out; and then, later in the day, Kathryn was busy with a fuller than usual catering schedule.

Sometimes, if pressed, she agreed to do two meals in one evening if the second customer ordered her chicken casserole which could be made a day ahead. But getting everything prepared on time was still a struggle because there were some items that could not be made in advance.

She was in and out all day buying groceries and running errands, and each time she came home, she found herself looking up and down the street for Nick's Porsche. But if he visited her downstairs neighbour, Kathryn did not see him. By Tuesday afternoon, she was beginning to think that it might not be necessary to talk to Julia about him after all.

Then, when she came home from delivering the second of the dinners she had made for that evening, she saw the Porsche parked across the street; and because she had been lulled into thinking that he might be gone for good, she was almost as startled as she had been the first day Nick had appeared on her stoop.

Her stomach did a flip flop, and she hesitated for several minutes before she could make herself climb the front steps. Then she put her ear to the door and listened for voices before she dared to enter.

It was only when she was safely in her flat behind a locked door that the foolishness of her actions occurred to her. This was her own house and she was sneaking around like a thief. A stranger watching from the street might have been justified in calling the police.

She went to the stove to heat herself some water for tea and resolved to knock on Julia's door early enough in the morning to make sure that she'd be at home.

Kathryn was downstairs before nine a.m. When Julia came to the door, her white hair was slightly mussed and she was buttoning the cuff of a neat silk blouse that looked as though it had been hastily tucked into her navy skirt. She was obviously preparing to go out, but Kathryn had no qualms about delaying her. She had caused Kathryn enough inconvenience in the last few days to deserve worse than a little interruption in her morning plans.

'I'd like to speak to you, Julia,' she said without preamble.

'My, my, Kathryn, of course. Please come in. You haven't knocked on my door in ages,' Julia said as she finished adjusting her blouse and backed away from the door.

She ushered Kathryn into her cluttered front room which was furnished with mostly Victorian pieces and had a comfortable long-lived-in look about it. All the tables and shelves were covered with mementoes of events far in the past.

Kathryn sat in her usual high-backed chair by the window and said, 'I think you know why I'm here.'

'You look so serious.' Julia made fluttering motions with her hands. 'I hope you haven't come to raise the rent.'

Kathryn looked up at the bird-like woman and motioned for her to sit. 'You know I wouldn't do that.'

But Julia continued to flutter. 'Then I don't know

what it could be. My brain isn't what it used to be, you know.'

Kathryn sighed in exasperation. No one she knew had ever been able to stay mad at 'The Little Widow Quimby' and she was no exception. She smiled and shook her head. 'Your brain is better than mine, and we both know it. Now would you stop hovering over me and have a seat?'

At Kathryn's words there was an immediate change in Julia's demeanour. Her flying motions stopped and she sat down and rested her hands quietly in her lap. The vague expression she'd been wearing changed into a wry intelligent smile and she sighed ruefully, 'You'll have to forgive me, dear. Since your grandmother passed away two years ago, there's no one in the world who expects sanity of me except you. Everyone else looks at my white hair and wrinkles and starts talking to me as though I were a two-year-old with a hearing aid. It's got so it's easier to act batty than to insist upon my dignity—and sometimes it's more fun, too,' she added with a twinkle in her eye.

Kathryn was reminded of the Cinderella outfit Julia had been wearing a few nights ago. It was in marked contrast to the neat skirt and blouse she had on now. 'I take it that explains the mink coat on a perfectly mild September evening?' she suggested.

'One gets so few chances to wear mink these days,' Julia sighed again. 'Your grandmother gave me that coat. She told me to wear it every chance I got— especially with the air conditioning they have nowadays.'

The statement was so typical of her grandmother that Kathryn had to swallow a lump in her throat. 'Gran could get away with anything,' she agreed.

'Helen knew how to live, and I thought she taught you,' Julia answered severely. 'After all, she was the one who brought you up.'

'But her method of relieving boredom was to go tearing off to Europe any time she felt like it. That sort of thing was only fun with her. And besides, I can't go running around the world and hold down a job, too.'

'You don't need to work and you know it,' Julia replied.

'So what am I supposed to do, sit home and twiddle my thumbs? As it is I have nothing to show for my life. It's long past time I settled down.'

'I suppose you're talking about Northrop Davis,' Julia said, 'but, as sure as I'm sitting here, I can bet that if Helen had been here, she'd have whisked you out of the country before he could have asked you for a second date. He's worse than the boy she saved you from marrying when you were in college.'

'Saved me from?' Julia made the statement as though it were old news, but it was new to Kathryn. It was as though a light went on in her head. She gave a small laugh and said, 'Do you know, Gran never said a word to me against Jerry. I never knew for sure that she wanted to break us up. She never said so. Do you realise that, if I had married him, I could have been the mother of teenage children by now? I let him go much too easily.'

'Better to let go *before* the marriage rather than after,' Julia replied. 'That boy had no staying power. If you had married him you'd probably be on your third or fourth husband the way your mother is. I didn't approve of your grandmother's tactics at the time—she never thought any man was good enough for you—but I understand better now. I'd take you to Europe myself, if I thought you'd go.'

'Wouldn't you be afraid I'd meet another Frenchman?' Kathryn asked, only partly in jest. 'Tell me, did Gran disapprove of Paul Danton, too?'

'As I recall, she said he was married.'

'He was getting a divorce before I met him.'

'Humph, I must say you haven't exactly been wise in your choice of men—except maybe this last one.'

'I thought you didn't like Northrop.'

'I wasn't talking about him.'

'Well you *should* be. There's nothing I can do about what happened in the past, but I'm in control of my own life now, and I'm sure everything will go fine from now on—with Northrop.'

'You always did see things through rose-coloured glasses,' Julia muttered, 'but I guess we all have to make our own mistakes. I suppose you think that once Northrop is married to you, he'll turn into some sort of a prince; but you'd better watch out—*you* may turn into a frog.'

'That's not funny, Julia. I've given this a lot of thought, and I realise that with Jerry and then with Paul, I let myself be swept off my feet. And where did it get me? Nowhere. Well, this time I'm not taking any chances. I want to have a child before it's too late and I want to give it a stable home life—not like the one I had.'

'But you had a good life with your grandmother——'

'I'm not talking about that. I mean *before* I went to live with her. My mother and father fought all the time until my father ran out on us. I'm not taking the chance that that might happen to my child.'

'All of life is a chance,' Julia informed her. 'You just have to look at your mother to see that. How's she doing with—what's she on now, husband number four, is it?'

'My mother seems happy with George in Phoenix,' Kathryn said defensively. 'Maybe this time it will work.'

The combination of a father who had run out on her and a mother who married at the drop of a hat had made Kathryn more than a little chary about marriage. She was never really surprised when her own affairs fell through.

'It would be about time something worked for her,' Julia said. 'She hasn't exactly set you a good example, I have to admit. By the way, may I ask what *she* thinks of your marrying Northrop—or haven't you bothered to tell her?'

'She has enough faith in me to tell me to use my own judgment. She'll come to Boston for the wedding, of course.'

'The least she can do,' Julia responded dryly. 'A real mother would at least want to meet the man first. She might find that she had a thing or two to say about him after all.'

'Mother doesn't interfere.'

'And I suppose you think I do,' Julia sighed. She got to her feet and drew herself up as far as her diminutive stature would allow. 'Your grandmother asked me to keep an eye on you, but I guess I haven't done much of a job. Now if you were marrying someone like Nick Varganin . . .'

'There's no question at all of that,' Kathryn interrupted hastily. She stood up and frowned down at the old woman. 'In fact, that's what I came to talk to you about before I got sidetracked. I want you to stop inviting him over here. It will just make trouble for me if you do.'

'Now why should it do that? He's an old friend of yours, isn't he?' Julia wrinkled her brow in what Kathryn sensed was feigned perplexity.

Kathryn sighed, 'You didn't really believe that story, did you?'

'No, dear. He isn't really the academy type. But he is a nice young man and one that I would encourage if I were you.'

'You don't understand——'

'Well, I don't want to pry, but maybe if you told me about it?'

'There's nothing to tell.'

'No, of course there isn't. I shouldn't have asked.'

Kathryn sensed Julia's hurt. 'No, that's OK. I mean, it's nothing so terrible——'

She paused and turned away to the window to consider. Julia acted so flighty these days that Kathryn tended to forget that she could be both sharp and discreet if she wanted to be. Perhaps the truth might be the best persuader.

She turned back to her elderly neighbour and said warningly, 'I'm telling you this in the strictest of confidence.'

'Of course, my dear.'

'OK then. As I'm sure you've figured out, Nick is not an old friend. We met a few weeks ago when I went to Block Island for a holiday. He seemed so nice and big and unthreatening that I . . . well I started to do things with him.' She looked to Julia for understanding.

'Yes, I can see how you would. He seems very nice to me, too. So what was the problem?'

'The problem was that things got out of hand. I still don't know how it happened, but we . . . well we . . . we became more than friends, if you know what I mean.'

She stopped because she thought she heard a distinct, 'Tsk, tsk.' She had let her eyes slide away from Julia's face as she told the embarrassing truth; and when she looked back, Julia smiled and said, 'I'm sorry, dear, I just didn't think you did that sort of thing.'

'I don't. I mean I didn't. I mean . . . Oh, Julia, I don't know why it was I did it! I went away to think about marrying Northrop and then I met Nick. I couldn't seem to stop myself. It was like nothing that has ever happened to me before. I know I never would have done it if I'd already been engaged, but——'

'But you were smart enough not to say yes to Northrop right away. What I don't understand is why you've said yes at all.'

Kathryn shook her head resignedly. Julia was determined not to see her point of view. 'I'm not going to try to talk you into giving Northrop a chance,' she said evenly. 'I've given up on that. But now that you know about Nick you can see why I can't have him hanging around here any more. He can ruin everything for me.'

'Now wait a moment, Kathryn. You talk about giving Northrop a chance, what about Nick? Has it occurred to you that he might be in love with you?'

Kathryn despised herself for the thrill of hope that went through her at the thought. It was impossible but yet ... 'Has he said anything to you?' she asked warily.

'Well, no——'

'I thought not.' Kathryn had to work to keep the disappointment out of her voice. 'You don't understand Nick at all. He only looked me up because he doesn't know anyone else in Boston. Once he gets on his feet, he'll forget I even exist. But in the meantime he's liable to ruin everything for me. How do you think it looks to have him going in and out of our house at all times of the day and night?'

'I've never known you to care very much about what people think,' Julia said stubbornly. 'And *I* think you underestimate yourself. You don't know how Nick feels.'

'Oh yes, I do,' Kathryn broke in. 'He and I have discussed marriage—in a theoretical way,' she hastened to add. 'He says he doesn't believe in it. He was married when he was younger and I guess it was pretty bad. Anyway, he made it very clear to me that he doesn't plan to try it again.'

'People have been known to change their minds——'

'I don't care if he does. I'm not taking any chances. I want to have a child, and for a child I need a stable marriage. That means Northrop, not Nick.'

She looked Julia straight in the eye to see that she had got her message across, but Juilia gave a sorrowful sigh and shook her head. 'Well, you know your own mind, and I would help you if I could, but I'm afraid it's impossible.'

'What do you mean impossible?'

'I've promised to help Nick find a flat and I can't go back on my word.'

'You mean that none of what I just told you makes any difference at all?'

'You're worrying too much about what people will think. If anyone asks, I'll say that Nick is an old friend of mine as well as yours and that he's visiting me. You'll find that the women will be too glad that you have no claim on him to question too closely, and all Northrop will want is his business at the bank.'

'But he isn't going to bank with Northrop——'

'Of course he is. It will look strange if he doesn't, don't you think?'

'No. Oh, I don't know.' Kathryn felt defeated on all counts. Nothing in the interview with her elderly friend had gone right. First she had learned things about her grandmother's interference in her life that she would rather not have known, and now she was losing ground she had never expected to cover.

'I suppose you intend to let him keep coming over any time he wants to?'

'Northrop or Nick?'

'You know very well who I mean.'

'I don't exactly get a lot of visitors these days that I shall start turning them away,' Julia said pointedly. 'I imagine he'll keep coming in—at least until we get him out of the hotel he's staying in. As a matter of fact, we're going flat hunting this morning.'

As she spoke, she went over to a wall mirror that was surrounded by old photographs and began to pat the waves of her white hair into order. The doorbell rang and both women jumped a little at the sound. Julia's cheeks took on a pink flush to match her blouse and she said with barely concealed excitement, 'That must be Nick now.'

If Kathryn had realized one moment sooner that Nick was coming, she would have made her getaway before he could arrive. But now she was trapped. She was annoyingly aware that her own pulse had accelerated in anticipation of seeing him, and she suspected that her own cheeks were as flushed as Julia's.

But Julia was acting like a schoolgirl going out on her first date, and Kathryn felt more like a truant about to be caught. Julia's actions showed more plainly than words the effect Nick had on her, and it was clear that he would not be turned away from her door.

In spite of herself, Kathryn stole a look in the mirror as she passed. For once, her dark hair was staying neatly in its topknot, and as she'd suspected, her cheeks were a tell-tale pink. She sighed at her inability to keep calm when Nick was around and followed Julia out into the hall. She looked longingly up the stairs towards escape, but she stood her ground as Julia opened the door.

Nick seemed to fill the door frame as he was silhouetted against the outside light. He wore a white polo shirt and khaki slacks—an outfit almost identical with Kathryn's own—and he glowed with vitality.

'Ah, good morning, ladies,' he said with a pleased look of surprise when he saw the two of them standing together.

'Good morning, young man. We were just talking about you, weren't we, Kathryn?' Julia said gaily.

'Were you now?' Nick's look of pleasure deepened to delight at her words, and Kathryn felt like one of a pair of hens greeting a rooster.

'One of us was trying to figure out how to get rid of you,' she said tartly.

'Now Kathryn, how ungracious of you,' Julia protested. 'What will Nick think of our Boston hospitality?' She made a clucking sound in her throat that reminded Kathryn even more of a hen. Then she motioned Nick to enter her flat. 'Come in a moment while I fetch my coat and bag.'

She disappeared inside in quest of her belongings, but Nick did not move at once to follow. He looked at Kathryn and seemed to be searching for something to say. Kathryn wanted to slip by him and go up to her flat, but for some reason she waited to hear him out.

'Look, I'm not trying to make trouble for you,' he whispered and gestured towards Julia's open door.

'The fact that you exist is trouble enough,' she hissed back.

He ignored her rebuff and went on earnestly, 'Well, I just wanted to tell you . . . to warn you that——'

He was interrupted by Julia who came out dressed in a navy jacket to match her skirt. She waved a small clutch bag at them and said, 'I'm ready, Nick.'

Nick did not finish his sentence. He smiled at Julia as though she had not interrupted anything and said, 'Very good. Shall we go?' He raised his eyebrows as Kathryn as though to say, 'Another time?' but Kathryn gave no hint of interest.

Her 'goodbye' was lukewarm to their more enthusiastic ones, and she headed back upstairs before they were out of the door. She wondered fleetingly what Nick had wanted to tell her, but she did not let herself dwell upon it for long. She had a dinner to prepare for that evening, and then the next evening was her weekly dinner out with Northrop and his business associates. She did not want or need to think about Nick.

One stray thought that did occur to her during the day was that she should have tried to tell Nick that Julia knew the truth about them. It was important that he did not tell anyone else the ridiculous story he had told Julia. The fiction about his going to the academy would not hold up for a minute with anyone else who had been there.

She thought about leaving him a note on Julia's door or trying to call him, but then she decided that it couldn't possibly be necessary. What harm could he do, after all?

The next evening she wished that she had called him. But by then it was too late.

Thursday evenings Northrop regularly had dinner with his broker, John Walters, and his lawyer, Mark Prentiss. When he and Kathryn had begun to meet seriously, he had invited her to meet them and they had invited their wives.

Since then it had become a regular sixsome, and Kathryn enjoyed it because she liked Lisa Walters, who was much younger than her husband, and Nora Prentiss, who was a kind, motherly sort of woman. Occasionally, other couples joined them, but usually their table was limited to six.

Their evenings were rather formal, and Northrop liked to have Kathryn dress accordingly. The new outfits she had bought were for these occasions.

She had also got into the habit of having her hair done on Thursdays so that, for at least twenty-four hours, it behaved. She refused to have her silky, shoulder-length hair cut to a more manageable length, and so she compromised by having it put into a neat chignon every week.

When Northrop called for her that evening, she
wore a sedate navy silk dress with white collar and
cuffs and a matching jacket. Northrop's pleased look
told her that he approved and his words confirmed it.
'You look absolutely regal this evening, my dear,' he
said. Her low heels made her an inch taller than he
and he had to reach up slightly to kiss her cheek.

She didn't ask about their dinner companions
because she assumed that she knew who they were. By
the time they got to the restaurant and she saw that
there was one extra guest, it was too late for her to do
anything but stand there.

She looked from Northrop's smiling face to Nick's
sardonic grin and she wanted to turn around and walk
right back out of the restaurant. For certain Northrop,
would learn who Nick really was before the night was
over, and all Kathryn could think was, 'My god, the
game is up.'

It had been one thing for Northrop to forgive her
for having an affair with some man they'd never see
again. It was quite another to find out that the man
was Nick. Even Northrop's generosity didn't go that
far.

If she could have, Kathryn would have made herself
disappear. As it was she pulled a smile from
somewhere and said weakly, 'Hello, Nick.'

Nick nodded to her. 'Hello, Kathryn.' His eyes went
over her neat hair and conservative dress and she read
amusement in his expression. 'You look very . . . um
. . . *nice* this evening.'

Kathryn's bare 'Thank you,' was covered by a more
enthusiastic Northrop. 'I invited Nick especially for
you,' he said in a pleased-with-himself voice. 'He
thought he'd be intruding, but I assured him that any
friend of yours would be welcome. He's also our
bank's newest and most prized client.'

Kathryn's smile dimmed a bit around the edges at

this latest bit of news, and her eyes told Nick exactly what she thought of it. 'I hope you haven't done any of this on my account,' she said evenly, knowing that he would get her meaning.

'It's all just good business,' Northrop answered her. He gestured towards the others who were standing around waiting to be acknowledged, and Kathryn belatedly greeted them.

She noticed that Lisa Walters seemed more animated than usual, and even sedate Nora Prentiss had a glow about her. The two women managed to sit on either side of Nick; and Kathryn ended up across the table from him where, unless she stared at her plate, she had to look right at him and watch him flirt with the two women.

She had never noticed before how much Lisa resembled an eager, ebony-coated spaniel, but the younger woman's short, black hair and large, bright, brown eyes, which rarely left Nick's face, looked distinctly puppyish that evening.

Nora Prentiss had the disadvantage of looking like a dowager Saint Bernard, but even she managed to get her fair share of Nick's attention.

Kathryn concentrated on getting as little of anyone's attention as she could. Her only salvation lay in hoping that no one would ask about the fictitious past she had shared with Nick.

But she might have known it was a forlorn hope. Northrop himself brought the subject up.

When there was a lull in the conversation, he smiled at Nick and Kathryn in turn and said, 'I understand that you were school friends, but I never asked when. Was it in college? You went to Smith, my dear, didn't you?'

Kathryn nodded and prepared for doom. In seconds Nick would mention the academy and it would be all over. Everyone at the table had gone to the academy at

one time or another, and there was no way at all that
Nick was going to get away with pretending he had
been there, too. She gave him a despairing look and
prepared for her fate.

But doom did not arrive. 'Yes, it was in college,'
Nick said, as though he'd been waiting for the
question all along. 'I was a couple of years ahead of
Kathryn and I went to Yale—you Harvard men will
have to excuse me.'

The men chuckled politely and he continued.
'Actually, I went out with a friend of Kathryn's,
Dottie McGraw. Whatever happened to Dottie, do
you know, Kathryn?'

'I . . . no . . . we haven't kept in touch,' Kathryn
managed. She'd been so sure that Nick was going to
mention the academy, that she couldn't believe he
hadn't. College? Yale? Where had he got that story?

'Oh, that's too bad. Dottie was a great little girl. I
thought you were good friends.' Nick smiled blandly,
but his eyes challenged her to keep up her end of the
story.

'Um, yes, we were.' Kathryn thought fast. 'She
lived across the hall from me in the dorm, but I don't
think she graduated. I had the impression that she
married you. It must have been someone else.'

'It must have been, or my memory's really shot,'
Nick grinned and the others laughed.

He seemed to be about to take the tale even further,
but Kathryn didn't trust herself to keep up with him.
He might think it was amusing, but her future was on
the line. To forestall him, she cleared her throat and
pushed her chair away from the table.

'If you'll excuse me, I need to go to the powder
room. I'll be right back.' She didn't look to see if the
others noticed her agitation but made her escape
before one of the other women could offer to join her.

In the ladies' lounge she sat on one of the couches,

laid her head back, and shut her eyes. Julia must have talked to Nick, or else he had come up with the story of his own. Whatever the case, he seemed to have thought up a foolproof plot. Smith girls did date Yale men, and no one would bother to check about Dottie McGraw. No one would even accuse Kathryn and Nick of being old flames. It was almost too perfect.

If Nick hadn't been the cause of all her trouble in the first place, she might even have been grateful. As it was, she decided that she would at least be a little less antagonistic towards him in the future.

When she had completely regained her composure, she checked out her appearance in the wide vanity mirror and prepared to return to the table. She was surprised that neither Lisa nor Nora had followed her to the lounge, but as soon as she left its sanctuary, she saw that someone had. Nick was waiting just outside the door.

She hadn't expected it and her guard went up immediately making her forget her resolutions to be nice to him. 'What do you want?' she asked suspiciously.

He smiled down at her and drawled, 'That's gratitude for you. I pull your irons out of the fire and that's all the thanks I get? I thought it was a pretty good story, if I do say so myself.'

'You might have warned me you were going to tell it.'

'*You* might remember that I did try to talk to you yesterday before I took Julia out flat-hunting. *You* wouldn't listen.'

It was true. He had tried to tell her something, but she had been too upset by her unsuccessful interview with Julia. And now she didn't want to be seen skulking around the ladies' room with him either.

'You're right,' she admitted hastily, 'and I even thank you; but we had better be getting back——

He grabbed her arm as she would have left him and pulled her back to face him. 'Wait a minute. I didn't follow you out here to bask in your warm thanks. If we know what's good for us, we'll go somewhere and really get our stories straight. If we're supposed to be old friends, there are lots of things we should know about each other.'

'I think we already know too much about each other, don't you?' Kathryn returned uncooperatively.

His smile was wry as he looked her up and down and answered, 'But not the kind of things we're supposed to know.'

Kathryn flushed. 'You can never resist a cheap shot, can you? I'd rather meet a snake.'

'OK, then.' He shrugged and turned away. 'It's all the same to me if we get caught in a lie. I don't stand to loose a thing.'

'Wait!' Kathryn plucked at his arm to stop him. 'OK, I'm sorry,' she said quickly, pretending that she didn't want to murder him for the supercilious look on his face. 'I was upset and not thinking clearly. Maybe it would be a good idea for us to meet. We can have lunch together—somewhere away from the city. As long as you promise not to . . . I mean, I don't want you to think . . .' Oh, why couldn't she finish a sentence any more?

He grinned at her and replied, 'Don't worry. Your virtue is safe with me. I like Davis, and I'm not the kind of guy who goes trespassing on another man's preserves—when I'm convinced they *are* his preserves.' His eyes glanced over her neat chignon and sedate navy dress, and this time Kathryn could tell that he was seeing the clothes and not the woman beneath.

She felt a flash of irritation at his unspoken criticism of her appearance. If she chose to dress for Northrop's taste, it was her own free choice. She was no one's 'preserves' except her own.

She opened her mouth to tell him so, but then she saw the gleam in his eye and changed her mind. He was obviously trying to get a rise out of her, and she had almost fallen in his trap.

Instead, she let his words roll right by her and went back to the main purpose of their conversation. 'I'm free tomorrow if you are. We can drive out into the country for lunch. I know of a good place to eat in Concord.'

'That sounds fine to me, but do you think we should drive together? Maybe we should take separate cars.'

'And maybe you should wear a moustache and a false nose! This isn't funny, Nick. You can pick me up at my flat, and if you're discovered you can say you're looking for Dottie McCrae.'

'McGraw,' Nick corrected her. 'See, we've got to get our stories straight.'

'McCrae, McGraw. I hate this, Nick.'

'So do I, but we've got to go ahead with it now that it's started. I didn't really believe in your engagement before tonight, but seeing you together with your friends with you looking and sounding like one of them has finally convinced me.

'So we'll go to lunch, work out a simple story, and then see each other only on the rare occasions that we can't avoid it. Does that sound fair enough to you?'

'Yes, of course. It's fine.' Kathryn's response lacked the appreciation and relief she should have been feeling. 'Now, I think we'd better get back to the others, don't you?' She turned and began to walk away.

But Nick detained her one last time. 'Shall I pick you up at . . . say eleven tomorrow then?'

'Yes, that will be fine. I have a dinner to cater and the earlier we get back the better.'

They walked back to the table together, and

Kathryn surprised herself with her coolness because, underneath, she was feeling anything but cool. She was sure that Nick had not intended to raise any doubts in her mind about her engagement to Northrop; but, nevertheless, he had.

She sat down next to her fiancé and tried as best she could to join in the conversation, but once doubt had invaded her mind, she couldn't make it go away; and for the rest of the evening, she was uncomfortable indeed.

All along, she had been assuming that, when she married Northrop, she'd be able to help him change into a more carefree person. They might live in his house and begin by seeing his friends, but soon they'd start to do more of the things Kathryn enjoyed.

Deep down where things mattered, she hoped to teach Northrop her love and enthusiasm for life. She hoped they could travel the way she had with her grandmother and show their children the world. She had said some of this to Northrop and he had seemed to agree, but now she couldn't help wondering if he had been humouring her. In the end, would she be the one to change?

She, after all, was the one who had bought new clothes and had got a new hairdo. For all she knew, Northrop planned to turn her into a carbon copy of his mother. It was an idea that did not bear thinking about, but in spite of herself, Kathryn did think about it.

Something Julia had said to her went flitting through her head. 'You think that once you marry Northrop, he'll turn into some sort of a prince, but you'd better watch out—*you* may turn into a frog instead.'

As the evening progressed, Kathryn kept looking at the navy sleeve and white cuff of her dress, and it began to seem as though it were the cuff and sleeve of some alien creature who was taking over her body. Could a simple change of style change the person beneath?

She tried to laugh off such an outrageous fantasy, but it was a thoughtful woman who returned to her flat that night, and she still hadn't shaken off her pensive mood when Nick arrived the next day to take her out to lunch.

CHAPTER FIVE

NICK seemed to sense her mood and made no great attempts at conversation as Kathryn guided him out of the twisting streets of Boston to the main road west of the city. It was not long before the dense suburban area was behind them and low green hills came into view. Already spots of autumn colour peeked through here and there as the swamp maples turned their premature red and yellow.

'This reminds me of when I was a boy,' Nick said musingly. 'Every Sunday we'd all get in the car and drive out to the country. In the summer we'd stop for ice cream, and in the autumn it was maple sugar and cider. During the winter we sometimes stopped at a lake—I forget the name—and we'd tramp around on the ice while Dad talked to the ice fishermen about what they were catching.'

Kathryn looked at Nick and sensed that he was trying to show her that he was no threat to her today. The picture he drew of himself as a little boy tended to take the sting out of the man.

Her own mood had softened in the lulling quiet of the drive, and she decided to try to forget her antagonism towards him and enjoy the outing. The purpose of the expedition was to learn more about each other's past, and Nick had made a good start.

'My grandmother and I did different things for different seasons,' she said. 'In the summer we stayed at a cottage at the shore, and in the winter we went to Palm Beach during my school holidays. But in the autumn we drove out into the country just the way you did.'

'There, you see, we might have met sometime in the

past after all—eating maple sugar candy at a roadside stand.'

'But you grew up in Connecticut, didn't you?'

'Yes, but our autumn drives took us far afield. We usually drove up towards Vermont on the Mohawk Trail.'

'So did we,' Kathryn said. 'The traffic used to come to a complete stop on the hairpin turns.'

'And I'd have to fight my sisters for the seat next to the window.'

'I always sat in front next to my grandmother.'

Nick chuckled. 'That really points up the difference between us, doesn't it?'

'I don't know. I think it would have been nice to have two sisters.'

'Not if they were both older than you and each thought she was the boss.'

'Poor Nick,' Kathryn laughed and her eyes met his. A wave of pure enjoyment and understanding passed between them, and Kathryn had to look away. She felt that she could almost see him as a boy. He would have been brawny even then and his hair would have been a bright flaxen blond. If only she could have a son like that——.

Kathryn, stop it! she admonished herself. Nick was giving her a questioning look, and she tired to collect herself and get back to the point of their talk. 'Um, where in Connecticut did you say you grew up?'

'Bridgeport—not smack in the middle of the town, but close to it.'

'Then we're both town kids.'

'With a difference. My father was a factory worker, not a Boston Brahmin.'

It was Kathryn's mother who was the Brahmin, but she didn't correct him. Instead she said, 'How un-American of you. You *did* say you managed to go to Yale, or was that just to make your story look good?'

Nick grinned. 'You sound as though you didn't believe it.'

'Well, it's just that——'

'I don't have the usual Yaley polish?' He gave a short laugh and said, 'I got there on a football scholarship. Oh, I had the grades—my father saw to that—but it was my brawn that breached the Ivy League walls.'

'You make it sound as though it wasn't worth the climb.'

'Well, I didn't exactly fit in—but I got a good education.'

'And you met our mutual friend, Dottie McGraw?'

'She came to a Freshman mixer.'

'My goodness, Dottie really got around. I never went to a Yale mixer in my life.'

'You didn't miss anything.'

'Oh, I don't know . . .' *I missed meeting you.* Kathryn didn't say the words aloud, but the thought suddenly hit her. What would have happened it she *had* met him in college instead of the weak-willed Jerry?

It certainly would have been possible. He was only two years older than she—he'd have been a junior to her freshman. Would she have appreciated Nick then—enough to defy her grandmother? Or maybe her grandmother would have approved of him. Julia did.

Kathryn didn't know what was the matter with her to have such thoughts, but at least she'd had the presence of mind not to say them aloud. This was the last day she was ever going to spend alone with Nick, and it was just as well.

She was relieved when they approached the town of Concord and she had to interrupt their reminiscing to guide him to the restaurant. She directed him through the beautiful centre of town with its white, clapboard churches and stone monument, to the old railway station which had been converted into a good French restaurant.

The food was plentiful and delicious, and after they ate, she showed him around the town which was historic not only for its part in the American Revolution, but also as the home of such nineteenth-century luminaries as Emerson, Thoreau, Hawthorne, and Louisa May Alcott.

They walked to the park surrounding Old North Bridge where the first shots of the Revolution had been fired, and they found a secluded spot where they could sit and enjoy the feeling of country and peace.

Kathryn felt that she was in much better control of herself by now. She sat on a spongy clump of dried grass while Nick sat a few feet away on a flat-topped boulder. While they had been walking, she had kept up a running commentary about Concord and its history, but now the two of them were silent as they basked in the warm September sunlight.

Kathryn lay back and tried to relax, but Nick remained seated and soon his gaze rested on her and began to make her feel uncomfortable again. She gave him a questioning glance and he smiled and said, 'This reminds me of why I had to come back to New England.' His hand made a sweeping gesture to encompass the surrounding field and the woods beyond. 'There's something inside anyone born here that cries out for snow in the winter, rain in the spring, and cool September afternoons in the sunshine.'

'How poetic.' Kathryn was unaccountably disappointed that he hadn't been thinking of her.

'You sound surprised.'

'One doesn't expect appreciation of nature from a tycoon.'

'I'm no tycoon and you know it. I'm the same man who watched the waves break on the rocks with you and raced across an island to watch the sun go down behind a lighthouse—have you so easily forgotten?'

'We both should try to forget everything about our past association, don't you think?' The truth was that Kathryn had been so overwhelmed by the physical bond that had sprung up between them on the island that she tended to forget everything else. Even while he admired the scenery, she was aware only of him sitting so close that she could touch him if she wanted to.

'I'm never going to forget anything about that island, Katie me darlin'.' His voice took on an exaggerated brogue.

When Kathryn would have protested, he put up his hand and added, 'But no mention of it will ever pass my lips, I promise.'

'I wish you would keep that promise now.' Kathryn straightened up into a sitting position and crossed her legs Indian fashion. 'We came here to talk about our *fictitious* past, remember?'

'Ah yes, our *fictitious* past. Once upon a time . . .' He broke off and gave her a considering look. Then he continued, 'Once upon a time there was a jaded man and a cowardly woman who met too late in life. They wished that they had met when they were young enough to take a chance on each other, but they did not. Now the man was past believing in miracles and the woman was choosing to marry for security. They met, kissed, and went their separate ways. The end. That's about it, wouldn't you say?'

'No——'

'Oh, yes it is. Just try to tell me that you're not sitting there wanting me as much as I want you.' His eyes pinned her to the ground, and she couldn't look away. Neither could she answer him.

It was Nick who finally broke the spell. His eyes released her and he looked off towards the woods. 'But that's all beside the point, isn't it? Things are the way they are and we can't change them. We just have to arrange the past a little more neatly.'

'Look, Nick, this whole thing was your idea. If you don't like it——' Kathryn broke off and made a move to get to her feet.

Nick put a hand on her arm to stop her. 'Don't be so hasty. We came out here for a reason, and let's get on with it. I believe that eons, before lunch, we were discussing good old Dottie McGraw and how she and I met.'

'We went through that already,' Kathryn said impatiently, but she settled back on the grass. 'It was at a Yale mixer.'

'Ah yes, were you there?' His question was facetious, and it immediately lightened the atmosphere between them.

'No. I had a cold that week, but Dottie told me all about it.' Kathryn gave him a begrudging smile.

'Did she now? And what else did she tell you?'

'That you were a football hero.'

'True. What else?'

'Hm . . .' That was all that Kathryn knew, but she could embroider as well as anybody. 'As I recall, she did nothing but brag the whole time she went out with you. She acted as though every touchdown you made was her own.'

Nick laughed out loud, and the last bit of tension left the air. 'Good old Dottie. So she said I made touchdowns, did she? If you ever see her around town, you'll have to take her up on that story. I was a tackle—all four years. I never even got my hands on the ball.'

'And all these years, I thought she'd snagged herself a quarterback. So much envy for nothing.' Kathryn gave an exaggerated sigh and realised that she was getting close to believing the story herself. 'Good grief,' she said, 'I'm starting to believe that Dottie really existed. I'd better watch it. Maybe you'd— better tell me something about your real past before we get into a hopeless tangle. Tell me, did you start your own business as soon as you got out of school?'

Kathryn asked the question innocently and she was surprised when the laughter left Nick's face and his eyes took on a faraway look. 'No, I went to work for my father-in-law.'

'Oh.' Kathryn didn't know what to say. She knew that his marriage had ended unhappily, and she had never meant to bring the subject up.

'I'm sorry——' she began.

But Nick interrupted. 'That's OK. It's not that bad. Marlene liked football heroes, too—and so did her dad. She and I got married as soon as I graduated, and I figured I was the luckiest guy in the world.'

He paused and picked up a twig and started rolling it between his fingers until it snapped. Then he threw it away and continued, 'The only trouble was, as far as my father-in-law was concerned, I couldn't stop being a football hero. I wanted to learn to manage the business, but all he thought I could do was take customers out to lunch.'

He shrugged his shoulders as though to show it didn't matter any more. 'I felt like I was going nowhere with him, so I decided to move out West and get a fresh start. *He* understood, but Marlene wouldn't go. She liked the life she had and wouldn't leave it. I figured she'd follow me out, but she never did. The next thing I knew, she filed for divorce and married a nice safe guy who would never give her a hard time. I wished her luck.'

Nick stopped abruptly and, when he went on, his tone had lightened considerably. 'My mistake, I guess, was in trying to change her. We were never really suited to each other. Anyway, the whole mess cured me of the urge to ever try it again. Married life is too hard to get out of once you've got in. Once was more than enough for me.'

Kathryn tried to give him an understanding smile, but her attempt was half-hearted at best. She knew that his words were not aimed at her, but she had the sinking feeling that they fitted. Hadn't Nick accused her, only a few minutes ago, of marrying for security? And hadn't she had her own doubts the evening before about Northrop's possible desire to change her into something she wasn't sure she wanted to be?

She felt the need to defend her position, even though it might not be under attack. 'One bad marriage doesn't make the whole institution a failure,' she declared. 'Where would we be if our parents hadn't got married?'

'Illegitimate.' He grinned and stood up. 'I'm sorry. I didn't mean to imply that all marriages were bad. You and Davis may be the lucky ones. Anyway, I'd be the last person to stand in your way. I think I still owe you an apology for the boorish way I behaved before I understood your situation.'

'That's all right,' Kathryn murmured.

But it was not all right. Nothing was. Nick said that he didn't want to be in her way, but as he stood above her, 'in her way' was exactly where he was. He might not want marriage and he might not want *her*, but he was making it impossible for her to want anyone else.

The whole day had conspired to make her realise that she wanted this man. He hadn't really said much about his wife, but Kathryn could see that her desertion had wounded him deeply. The hurt feelings that she knew he was keeping inside made her want to comfort him and show him that all women were not fickle.

But if she did what she wanted to do—if she stood up and put her arms around him and told him how she felt—she'd be proving that he was right. She'd be as fickle as his Marlene. It was a no-win situation.

So she stood up, but she made no move towards

him. Instead, in the easiest voice she could manage, she said, 'Apology accepted.' Then she turned her back on him and began to stretch the muscles in her back that had become cramped from sitting on the ground.

When she felt she was safe from throwing herself in his arms, she turned around and said, 'It's late. Don't you think we'd better be getting back to town?'

But a strange smile appeared on Nick's face as he watched her, and he put his hands on his hips and looked at her wonderingly. 'I just realised something,' he said. 'You remind me a little of Marlene.'

He held up his hand when she would have objected. 'It's not your face or body or anything like that. It's the way you move—the way you turned around just then. You looked like a queen. It's as though you know your place in the world and never doubt it. I bet that's what caught my eye when we met—nothing conscious mind you—but I always was a sucker for class. I guess I still am.'

The way he said the word 'class' was not a compliment, and Kathryn had never felt less like a queen. 'I think that what's inside a person counts a little bit more than the way she walks, don't you?' she asked.

His grin was back and he took a step towards her. 'I wasn't putting you down. I *like* the way you move.' He reached out a hand to touch her arm, but then he drew away as though the contact burned him.

They stared at each other and Kathryn knew that if she made one motion towards him, they'd be in each other's arms. But she didn't. She couldn't move.

Finally, he cleared his throat and put his hands in his pockets—out of harm's way? 'Don't pay any attention to me. That was a dumb thing to say.' He looked at his watch. 'And you're right, it *is* getting late. It will be three o'clock before we get home, and I have a late afternoon appointment.'

Kathryn somehow doubted his appointment. They had stopped at the brink and they both knew it. She had to practically run to keep up with him as he walked back to the car.

She arrived breathless and decided to make light of their headlong flight. 'Whew! I *do* have to make a dinner tonight, but I'm not in *that* much of a hurry.' She leaned against the hood to catch her breath and then sank gratefully into her seat when Nick opened the door.

Nick climbed in on his side and quirked a smile. 'Believe me. We were in a hurry.'

Kathryn wanted to ask why, but she caught his look and decided not to pretend to be dense. They had had a choice and they'd made it. It had been the right choice and she knew it—didn't she?

They said little to each other on the drive back to Boston, and Kathryn found herself watching his hands on the wheel and his thighs as they worked the pedals. He was wearing his khaki slacks and a blue dress shirt with the sleeves rolled up to the elbows.

She could see his muscles work under the material of his slacks, and she was fascinated by the way the sun slanted through the window to turn the fine blond hair on his forearms to gold.

Kathryn swallowed and realised that she wanted him so much at that moment that it was all she could do to keep herself from reaching over to touch him. Now that they had agreed to part, now that he had shown his determination to stay away from her, she wanted him more than any man she had ever met. She had to be crazy.

The turnabout in her feelings was so unlike her that she began to question her assumptions about everything—including Northrop and marriage. She thought she knew what she wanted, what she needed. It was marriage, a child, and security for that child. Nick offered her none of these. Was the love she felt for him strong enough to make up for what she'd be giving up?

Love!?!

Kathryn stopped herself on that thought and risked a glance at Nick. The idea was so sudden she was afraid she'd said it out loud. But his expression was grim, and she sensed that he was alone in some world he didn't like. She tried to turn her own thoughts away from the direction they'd been heading, but it was too late. She had come to the brink of realisation and she couldn't stop its conclusion.

I love him, she thought a little wildly. *All the things I thought I felt for him on the island were real. I love him!*

She'd been crazy to come out to the country with him, to listen to him speak of his family, and to hear the unhappiness in his voice when he spoke of his ex-wife. Their meeting was supposed to have protected her engagement to Northrop, not endangered it.

But it no longer made any difference what their intentions had been because the day had had the opposite effect. She couldn't marry Northrop now.

It was all right to marry a man you didn't love, provided you could be loyal to him and provided there was at least the possibility that love would grow. But it was not all right when you loved another man.

Blast you, Nick! Why did you have to come along now? A few years ago I would have loved you and not cared about marriage. A few years from now, I'd have had a couple of kids in tow and would have been safe from you. But here you are now and what am I going to do? How am I ever going to have a family—grow them like potatoes?

She must have muttered something aloud because Nick came out of his deep thoughts and looked over at her. 'I'm sorry, did you say something?'

'No, oh no. I was just . . . thinking.'

'Yes, so was I,' Nick smiled as though only half-seeing her and turned his attention back to the road.

His words night have been an opening gambit, but they weren't. The silence closed over them again like a blanket and Kathryn was free to pursue her own thoughts. They weren't particularly pleasant.

She was going to have to break her engagement to Northrop, and it wasn't going to be easy. The only thing that made her feel better about it was the insight she'd had the evening before. If he really wanted a carbon copy of his mother, Kathryn would never fit the bill and she knew it. Perhaps it was for the best after all.

Perhaps. Meanwhile, the man she loved sat a few inches away from her, and for the life of her, she couldn't come up with a thing to say to breach the wall between them. If she just came out and said, 'Nick, I'm afraid I love you,' he'd be sure to think that she had gone out of her mind.

So she said nothing until they approached the city and she had to give him directions. Then, too soon, they were at her door, and he didn't ask to come in. He stood stiffly in the front hall and his words hit her like a blow.

'I've been thinking all the way home, and I've come to the conclusion that the best thing I can do for you and for myself is get out of your life. This has been one hell of a day. If we'd been in a less public place, I don't think anything would have made me keep my hands off you. As it was, I almost lost control. And as long as I keep seeing you, that's not going to change.'

'But you didn't do anything,' Kathryn broke in.

'No, but the point is I wanted to. I still do.' His eyes drank her in, but the look on his face was angry rather than passionate, and Kathryn didn't dare interrupt again.

'What I'm trying to say is that I don't trust myself with you, and the way I see it there's only one solution. I'm going to keep out of your way from now on. Boston is a big city, I'll lose myself in it.'

He stopped speaking as though he'd run out of words, and for a moment they just stared at each other. It was obviously a prepared speech, but unfortunately he hadn't planned a good exit line.

Kathryn couldn't have helped him if she'd tried. It was so much the opposite of what she wanted him to say, that she was struck as dumb as he.

His finish was lame and awkward. 'Well, goodbye and good luck with Davis. And I'm ... sorry.' He reached out as though to shake her hand, seemed to see the inappropriateness of the gesture, and turned and walked quickly and rather heavily out of the door.

Kathryn put out a hand to stop him, but he didn't see it. 'Wait, Nick, you don't understand,' she began, but he didn't listen. As she watched in complete disbelief, he walked down the steps and got into his car. It couldn't be happening, but it was. Just as she'd realised she wanted him, he was going away—for good.

'Nick,' she called out once more, but he was already driving away. She stood looking out at the street for a long time. Then, feeling like a sleep walker, she went up to her flat. She walked over to the window with some crazy idea of willing him to return, but not even a pedestrian passed by on the pavement below. Nick was gone and there was no calling him back.

Double blast and damn you, Nick. You might at least have waited to hear what I had to say!

She turned away from the window and might have gone into terminal depression except she had a meal to prepare for that evening. For once she was glad that it was the most complicated dinner on her menu.

She gathered the ingredients for the main course and began to chop and mix and mash with a fervour that would have ruined a more sensitive dish. But like all her meals, it was not called foolproof for nothing. It survived the worst she could do to it, and by seven o'clock, she packed it up and delivered it right on time.

She returned home to a bigger than usual mess to clean up, but even this she was glad to do. If she ever needed to keep herself occupied, this was the time. Soon she'd have to sit down and decide what to do about both Northrop and Nick, and most of all, herself—but not yet, not yet.

It seemed that every time she found a man, she lost him—whether through her own doing or someone else's. It had been the same since her father had left her when she was six years old. Was there something wrong with her that she couldn't stay with a man?

Again it occurred to her that she might be just like her father—and her mother, too—a person who could not hold on to a relationship. As always when the thought came to her, it made her shudder.

She got out some cleanser and scrubbed the counters and the sink until her arms ached. It had been an absolutely frustrating day, and she wanted to be very tired before she tried to sleep. She didn't think it was possible for anything worse to happen to her.

She was wrong, of course. Worse could happen, and it did.

All night long she had terrible dreams, and she awoke very early the next morning feeling as though she'd got no rest at all. To top it off, as soon as she got up she felt sick to her stomach.

'Just what I need,' she groaned and ran to the bathroom.

At first she thought it was the flu, but it went away by mid-afternoon and returned the next morning. After a few days of the same pattern, even Kathryn, who rarely gave much thought to such matters, figured it out.

Her cycle was so irregular that she never kept track

of her periods, but she didn't think she'd had one since her holiday. It seemed impossible, but she was pregnant.

Clarice Benedict, who was an old schoolfriend as well as her doctor, confirmed it. 'Congratulations, Kathy. I thought you might have a hard time conceiving, but it looks like I was wrong. I'd say you're about six weeks pregnant.'

'I don't believe it. You said it would take me a year or more to conceive.'

'Even we experts can be wrong. In this case, I'm glad that I was.'

'You're absolutely sure? I mean, there can be no mistake?'

'Tests can be wrong at this early stage, but with your other symptoms, I'd say we could be ninety-nine per cent sure.'

'Wonderful.'

Clarice looked at Kathryn sharply and seemed finally to realise her dismay. 'I thought you'd be delighted. Weren't you just in here a few months ago making sure you'd be able to *have* a child? At your age, and with your history, I'd say you and Northrop are amazingly lucky—even if it is a few weeks before the wedding.'

Kathryn shut her eyes and admitted, 'It's not Northrop's child.'

'Oh.' Clarice looked nonplussed for a moment, but then she broke out in a grin. 'Why, Kathryn, I never thought you had it in you. I must say I found Northrop rather stuffy myself. Who's your new man?'

Kathryn suddenly wished she'd gone to a strange doctor rather than her friend. She really wasn't up to explanations. 'It's not a new man. I mean, it's over. It was never supposed to last. I didn't *plan* to get pregnant.'

'Did you plan *not* to?' Clarice asked dryly.

'Of course I did. I may be a little slow, but I'm not stupid.'

'No, only human. Some precautions fail no matter how careful we try to be.'

'Yes, well, that must be what happened,' Kathryn agreed. Then suddenly she remembered. There had been one time and only one. It had been the insane night Nick had made love to her in the back of his car. There hadn't been enough time to use anything.

She looked at Clarice and asked, 'You don't think one slip-up could have done it, do you? I mean, you told me it could take years.'

'That's it, blame the doctor. We both know it takes only one time—if it's the right time.'

'Or the wrong time.' Kathryn shut her eyes. 'What am I going to do, Clarice?'

The doctor sobered. 'I'm sorry, Kathy. I shouldn't joke, but I was so delighted for you that I'm having a hard time realising that this is not a happy occasion. Have you thought about what you plan to do? Will you have the child?'

Up until that point, Kathryn hadn't thought beyond her morning sickness and her incredulity. Words like 'precaution' and 'pregnancy' had made it sound more like a disease.

It was the word 'child' that finally woke her up to what was really happening to her and it brought a smile to her face for the first time in days. Soon that smile became a grin.

She looked at Clarice and laughed. 'Good heavens, Clarice, it just hit me, I'm going to have a *baby*!'

'Yes, that *is* what we were discussing,' Clarice agreed.

'I mean *I'm* going to have a baby. *Me*, the person who was afraid she'd never get a chance to be a mother. *You* may have two kids already, but *I'm* going to have a *baby*!'

'I take it that you've decided to keep it?'

'*Keep* it? My god, I must have been blind! Of course I'm going to keep it. I'm going to cherish it.' The picture of a tow-headed miniature version of Nick flashed through her mind. 'A baby is exactly what I needed, only I was too blind to see it. Who needs men?'

'You did at some point in all this,' Clarice answered wryly.

But Clarice's sarcasm couldn't dim Kathryn's excitement. She was a woman who had suddenly seen a vision.

By the time she left Clarice's office, she knew what it was like to fly without wings. She couldn't believe she'd been so dense for so long. Marriage was all well and good—if you found the right man—but it was not, after all, necessary in order to have a baby.

She'd been too much of a coward to *plan* to have a child outside marriage, but she knew that millions of women brought their children up alone—whether they wanted to or not. And most of them did a good job of it. There was no reason in the world that she couldn't do as well.

She walked out of the medical building, and towards home with her mind already busy with plans. 'Let's see, I'll turn Gran's old room into a nursery. I'll have to paint the walls. And Julia won't mind if I keep the pram behind the stairs . . .'

But the thought of Julia brought her back down to earth. She'd have to tell Julia, and her mother in Phoenix, and most important of all, she hadn't yet broken her engagement to Northrop. She was sorry now that she'd put off talking to him.

Her eye caught sight of a telephone kiosk, and she decided that there was no time like the present to get an unpleasant task over with. She called him at the bank, but he had already left for home. She looked at her watch and saw that it was four-thirty.

with 12 Romances Free

your welcome gift from Mills & Boon

Love, romance, intrigue...all are captured for you by Mills & Boon's top selling authors. By becoming a regular reader of Mills & Boon's romances you can enjoy twelve superb new titles every month plus a whole range of special benefits: your very own personal membership card, a free monthly newsletter packed with recipes, competitions, exclusive book offers and a monthly guide to the stars, plus extra bargain offers and big cash savings.

As a special introduction we will send you 12 exciting Mills & Boon Romances and an exclusive Mills & Boon Tote Bag FREE when you complete and return this card.

At the same time we will reserve a subscription to Mills & Boon Reader Service for you. Every month, you will receive twelve of the very latest novels by leading Romantic Fiction authors, delivered direct to your door. And they cost just the same as they would in the shops – postage and packing is always completely Free. There is no obligation or commitment – you can cancel your subscription at any time.

It's so easy! Send no money now – you don't even need a stamp. Just fill in and detach this card and send it off today.

plus the exclusive
Mills & Boon
**TOTE BAG
FREE**

Dear Susan,

Your special Introductory offer of 12 Free books is too good to miss. I understand they are mine to keep with the Free Tote Bag.

Please also reserve a Reader Service Subscription for me. If I decide to subscribe, I shall, from the beginning of the month following my free parcel of books, receive 12 new books each month for £13.20, post and packing free. If I decide not to subscribe, I shall write to you within 10 days. The free books will be mine to keep, in any case.

I understand that I may cancel my subscription at any time simply by writing to you. I am over 18 years of age.

Name _____
(BLOCK CAPITALS PLEASE)

Address _____

_____ Signature _____

Postcode _____

2A6T

STAMP NEEDED

To Susan Welland
Mills & Boon
Reader Service
FREEPOST
P.O. Box 236
CROYDON
Surrey CR9 9EL.

SEND NO MONEY NOW

Without letting herself falter, she hailed a taxi and was deposited outside his house before she could have second thoughts. She rang the doorbell and was surprised when Loraine Davis answered the door herself.

'Why hello, Kathryn. How nice of you to look in. Won't you come in?'

'I just called to speak to Northrop if he's at home,' Kathryn said, not moving from the door.

'Why no, though he should be soon. Would you like to come in and wait for him?' She motioned for Kathryn to enter.

Kathryn didn't want to, but she found herself following Loraine into the parlour at the back of the house. She accepted a cup of tea, and then to her horror, she felt herself becoming nauseous. Before she could think of what she was doing, she had confessed her condition to Northrop's mother.

Loraine looked momentarily embarrassed, but soon a pleased expression appeared on her face. 'I suppose it is somewhat premature, but then it is what we all want, isn't it?'

Kathryn shut her eyes as she told the older woman that the child was not Northrop's.

There was a silence in the room, but then Loraine cleared her throat and said, 'I'm sorry, my dear——'

But Kathryn broke in. 'No, I'm the one who's sorry. It was unforgivable of me to come and tell you like this. I didn't plan to tell Northrop anything except— well, that I couldn't marry him after all. Please try to forget that I came.' She moved to get up, but just then the telephone rang. It was Northrop telling his mother that he wouldn't be home for dinner.

Loraine Davis turned from the phone to Kathryn and smiled sadly. 'It seems that your news will have to be postponed. Would you care to have dinner with me? There is always plenty of food.'

But Kathryn could see the strain behind Mrs Davis's pleasant countenance, and she wished heartily that she had never come at all. 'Thank you, but I think I'll just be getting home. It has been a tiring day.'

The two women walked to the front of the house together, and then, to Kathryn's surprise, Mrs Davis stopped her at the door. The older woman hesitated for a moment, and then she said, 'I don't want you to take this the wrong way, but before you tell Northrop or anyone else, would you please consider something for me?'

'Well, yes, of course.' What else could Kathryn say?

Loraine Davis hesitated again and then began slowly, 'This house needs children.' She gestured at the empty expanse behind her. 'The trouble is that Northrop is a very self-sufficient man. If he doesn't marry you, he may not even look for anyone else. I'm not asking you to deceive him, but perhaps your child might have a place in this house after all? No one would have to know the truth but us.' Her eyes begged for Kathryn's understanding.

Kathryn was stunned by the suggestion, even as she understood where it had come from. The two of them wanted the same thing—a child. But it was impossible.

'I'm sorry.' She shook her head. 'I do understand, but it wouldn't be right. And who knows, Northrop may surprise you and find someone else. He found me, didn't he?'

'Yes, of course.' Loraine Davis drew herself up, and it was as though the scene had never taken place. They said their polite goodbyes and Kathryn was back on the street feeling as though she had gone through the wringer.

She walked slowly home and hoped that her interview with Northrop would not be quite so harrowing. She had assumed all along that he was no more in love with her than she was with him, but after her talk with his mother, she wondered if anyone's assumptions about another person were ever correct.

She worried much about telling Northrop, but a few days later when she did, she found that he made it easy for her. She suspected that Loraine had prepared him, but she couldn't help but be grateful.

It was only when she handed him back his ring that he seemed to pause for a moment as though considering what it meant. He fingered the ring and said, 'I think I realised from the start that we weren't really suited to each other, but I am fond of you. I will take back this ring, but I want you to know that I am still your friend. If you ever need anything——' He left the thought unfinished, but the promise was there.

'Thank you, Northrop,' Kathryn answered simply. She almost wished at that moment that she could have loved him. He might be a little pompous, but he was a good man. If she hadn't met Nick, she and Northrop might have done all right with each other.

But she had met Nick, and the consequences of that meeting were now controlling her life—even if he had disappeared from the scene.

Her talk with Northrop occurred in her flat, and when he left there was such a sad feeling of gloom about the place she decided that she needed to get outside. She realised that her first happy feelings about the baby had been completely swamped by her need to break her engagement.

But now that that sorry task was accomplished, it was time to banish all the gloom and bring gaiety back into the Kathryn Gardner Lawrence establishment. After all, she was going to have a baby!

It was late afternoon, and unfortunately, the September sunshine had given way to rain, but she decided to ignore the elements and go for a walk in the Public Gardens. She put on a raincoat and began to hum as she left her flat and went down the stairs and out of the door. She had no catering job for that evening, and suddenly she felt as free as a bird.

She lifted her face to the misty sky and hugged herself as she walked. The euphoria she felt now that the burden of breaking her engagement was behind her showed her quite clearly how heavily the possibility of hurting Northrop had been weighing on her mind. But now it was over. All her ties to anything unpleasant were in the past.

She stopped to peer over the bridge in the Gardens and laughed out loud, heedless of what anyone might think of her. 'I'm a liberated woman,' she cried to the pigeons on the lamppost.

If a niggling thought at the back of her mind asked, 'What about the father?' she paid it no heed. Nick Varganin had put himself out of her life, and she was going to keep him there. Who needed men?

CHAPTER SIX

THE one sad note in Kathryn's walk was that her grandmother would not be alive to see her great-grandchild. Kathryn knew that her mother in Phoenix would *accept* the news that her daughter was having a baby without benefit of a wedding ceremony, but her grandmother would have *understood*. Was there anyone else she could say that about?

As if in answer to her question, the curtain in Julia Quimby's front room fluttered just as Kathryn came up the walk. She waited inside the door, and sure enough, Julia came out of her flat a few seconds later.

'I saw you go out in all that rain, and I thought you might like a cup of tea when you got back. You must be chilled to the bone.'

Kathryn had barely noticed the weather, but she recognised her neighbour's curiosity to learn what had been going on, and she decided to satisfy it. Julia was the only person left in Boston to whom she felt she owed an explanation.

She followed Julia into her flat and waited only until she was seated with a teacup in her hand before she said, 'You'll be delighted to know, Julia, that I have broken my engagement to Northrop.'

If she expected Julia to react with shock, she was disappointed. The elderly lady digested the information as she took her own seat across from Kathryn and then said, 'Humph, I knew you'd come to your senses eventually.'

Kathryn smiled at Julia's 'I told you so' manner and decided to get it all over with at once. 'Yes, I have come to my senses,' she agreed easily. 'I've also come to something else. I found out this week that I'm going to have a baby.'

Julia looked at her over her teacup and gave another, 'Humph. I suppose you expect me to be shocked,' she grumbled. 'You young people always think you've invented something new, but it's a story older than time.'

Kathryn smiled at being called a 'young person' but Julia was going on, 'You're the one who will be shocked a few months from now when you see how much work there is to being a mother. I suppose Nick is the father?'

'As far as I'm concerned, there is no father,' Kathryn said. 'This will be my child and mine alone.'

Julia made a face at Kathryn's rather inaccurate statement, but she must have decided to ignore it because her next words showed that her mind had already gone on to other things. 'I imagine you'll be wanting me to babysit,' she said grumpily.

Kathryn grinned, not at all fooled by Julia's tone. She'd seen the light of hope and speculation behind the elderly lady's eyes the minute she'd said the word 'baby', and she knew that she'd have a hard time keeping Julia away from the child.

'I may let you visit, but it will be on an appointment-only basis,' she declared. 'I will not have my child spoiled.'

'Spoiled! You'll be singing a different tune by the time you're getting up every night for a two o'clock feeding,' Julia muttered. 'Let's just hope it's a girl, since it's going to be brought up by women.'

Kathryn put down her teacup and went to kiss Julia's cheek. She hadn't realised how much she'd counted on her elderly friend's support until it had been offered.

'Thanks, Julia,' she said simply. She returned to her flat feeling that she was one of the luckiest unmarried mothers around.

*　　*　　*

She had several good days before the next obstacle appeared in her path—almost enough time for her to think that she was home and dry. She thought about Nick at night when she couldn't help herself, but during the day, she kept herself too busy to wonder where he had gone.

He hadn't gone far. He appeared at her doorstep one morning later that week and he was as mad as a thunder-cloud. Kathryn had walked down to the store for a carton of milk, and she found him sitting on the stoop when she returned. She looked over at Julia's window, but for once, she detected not the slightest flutter.

One part of Kathryn couldn't help but be delighted to see Nick, but the more discerning part noted that, as he sat in front of her door, he had the distinct aura of a great blond grizzly bear—and an untamed one at that.

She expected him to rise as she mounted the first stair, but he remained seated and she backed off. He was looking at her as though she were some strange apparition, and she wasn't sure what would come out of his mouth.

What came out of hers was a very uncertain, 'Why, hello, Nick. I didn't expect to see you here.'

He continued to glare at her for moments that seemed like hours, and then his words parroted hers. 'Why, hello, Nick, I didn't expect to see you here. Like hell you didn't! You had it all planned from the start. I was really some kind of a fool to be taken in by that ladylike act of yours!'

Kathryn stared at him open-mouthed. 'I don't know what you're talking about, Nick, and I don't think you do either. Would you please get off my steps so I can pass?'

But he didn't budge. He planted his elbows on his

knees, put his chin in his hands, and grinned evilly at her. 'I don't know what you're talking about, Nick,' he mimicked her again. Then his grin disappeared and he practically sneered at her. 'You can lay off the act. Maybe it will clear things up for you if I tell you that I saw your precious Northrop this morning.'

So now he knew that she wasn't engaged any more. It could hardly account for such anger. 'I suppose he told you that I broke our engagement,' she said non-committally, 'but I fail to see what that has to do with you.' She looked up and down the street and was glad to see that there was no one within hearing distance.

He caught her glance and laughed aloud. 'Afraid the neighbours will hear? Well, they haven't heard anything yet.' He got to his feet and came down the stairs towards her.

But Kathryn was not going to submit to his bullying. 'I don't know what's the matter with you, but I don't intend to discuss it on the street.' She slipped past him and ran up the steps as he vacated them. She had her key ready and had turned the lock before he reached her.

They entered the hallway together, but she paid him no heed. She marched up the stairs and was at her door before she realised that he had followed her no further than the front hall.

As she turned to look down at him, he put a hand on the newel post and called out. 'Aren't you at all curious as to what your *ex*-fiancé told me?'

Kathryn looked at Julia's door, which she knew sheltered her interested neighbour and said, 'Not particularly.'

Nick laughed again as he, too, looked at Julia's door. 'Don't try to tell me that Julia knew nothing about this. She's as much a part of the plot as the rest of you.'

Kathryn shook her head. 'Plot? What plot? I don't

know what you're talking about.'

His laugh turned to a jeer. 'Well, then, I'll just have to enlighten you, won't I?'

'Wait!' Kathryn took two steps back down the stairs. 'Look, I don't know what this is all about, but there's no sense in us shouting out here. You can come inside.' She unlocked the door and stood waiting for him to join her.

He hesitated as though reluctant to accommodate her in any way, but finally he strode up the stairs, through her door, and into the middle of her living room.

As soon as she shut the door, he flung out his arms; and the words boiled up out of him as though he could contain them no longer. 'Do you know what it's like to go to a man's office expecting a business discussion and having him accuse you of moral turpitude— whatever the hell that is? To have him suggest that you do "the right thing" when you don't know what the hell's going on?

'I thought he was talking about my business, and I figured my accountant must have tried some fancy tax dodge. I sat there for ten minutes before I finally figured out that he was talking about you!'

He stopped his wild motions and pointed a finger at Kathryn.

She was standing by the closed door wondering if she'd let a wild man into her flat, and when he stopped speaking she was unready for a reply. All she could come up with was a weak, 'Me?'

He shook his head and laughed mirthlessly. 'My god, what an actress! And all the time I thought I lured you to *my* bed! You must have picked me out on the damned ferry boat. What were you looking for, the father of a future halfback?

'And then all that rot about marrying Northrop and having a family! You had me feeling so guilty for ever laying a hand on you that I was ready to leave Boston.

It was all part of your trap for me, wasn't it? You thought I'd do "the right thing" and marry you because I'd debased some sort of well-born lady. Well let me tell you this, it will be a cold day in *hell* before I let you spring that trap on me!'

'Trap! *Trap!*' Kathryn remained with her back to the door, but she had stopped feeling surprised or the least bit frightened by his outburst. If he was angry, she was furious.

'My god, I wouldn't have you on a plate if it was edged with gold! The nerve of Northrop to even *talk* to you. I didn't even tell him that I was pregnant, never mind who the *father* is. There's no way he could know that unless——' Her mind flew to the silent flat downstairs. 'My god, Julia! Blast her for interfering!'

Nick had listened to her with pure scepticism on his features, and when she finished, he clapped his hands as though he'd been watching an amusing play. 'What a performance. Outraged virtue at its best, and poor Julia the scapegoat for it all. I'm supposed to believe you and then get down on my knees and offer to make an honest woman of you, is that it? Well let me tell you this, you can slander my name to Timbuktu, but I won't be blackmailed into giving my name to a child I can't even be sure is mine!'

Kathryn was across the room in a flash. She raised her hand to strike him, only to find that she was still holding the container of milk she'd bought. The ridiculousness of hitting him with a carton of milk stopped her, but only for a second.

She brandished it in the air and cried, 'You stupid, conceited bastard, you! I wouldn't want any child of mine to have your name even if you *had* fathered it. But it's *not* your child. It's not *anyone's* child but *mine*. I'm going to have it, bring it up, and love it; and I don't need any stupid macho hulk to make things harder for me.

'Now get out of here before I . . . before I hit you with this milk! And don't you ever *dare* come back. Do you understand?'

She flung open the door and had to constrain herself from pushing him out of it. He stopped in the hall, as though to get in one last word, but she slammed the door in his face. After a moment, in which she held her breath, she heard his angry tread on the staircase and the slamming of the outside door.

Kathryn let out her breath and kicked the wall. Of all the unadulterated stupidity, his had to be the worst. To think for a minute that she'd ever try to trap a man into marrying her. The idea had gone out with the dark ages. She shuddered from head to toe with delayed reaction and brandished the milk carton again in the air. She wished she *had* hit him with it. It was the least he deserved.

Then the silliness of using a paper carton as a weapon finally came to her and she felt her lips twitch in a smile. She would be willing to bet that Nick had never been threatened with that particular weapon before.

Her stomach grumbled and she remembered why she had gone out for the milk in the first place. Clarice had given her something to take for her morning sickness, but she still needed to put food in her stomach in the morning, or she felt a bit queasy. She got down a bowl and some cereal and made herself eat even though she was still angry.

She ate two bowls of the crunchy flakes, and by the time she was on her second bowl, she'd stopped dreaming up suitable punishments for Nick and started thinking about the two other culprits in the morning's fiasco. Nick had not been in it alone.

Northrop had divulged information he'd had no right to pass on, and the source of that information— at least the crucial part of it—could only have been

Julia. That lady was the only person in the world who knew, for sure, that Kathryn and Nick had had an affair.

Kathryn got up from the table with the idea of going downstairs to share some of the misery with Julia, but then she stopped halfway to the door. The house had a quiet expectant feeling about it. She could bet that Julia was sitting in her front room right now, waiting to get her come-uppance.

Kathryn decided not to give it to her. There was nothing worse than to have to wait for the axe to fall, and right now that was what Julia was most certainly doing. Kathryn decided to make her wait a little longer, maybe even forever. She went over to the stove to boil water for some tea and then settled in her own chair by the window to think.

Unfortunately, or fortunately, for her, she was the kind of person who could never stay angry with anyone for long, and soon she began to see the humour in the situation.

Nick had looked like a great Russian bear as he'd stood flailing his arms about in the air. And the idea that she would try to trap anyone into marrying her was so ludicrous that even *he* would realise it soon enough and feel like an absolute fool. Why, when they'd left the island, she'd never expected to see him again. He knew that as well as she. When he cooled down, he'd probably want to shoot himself.

Kathryn smiled and put her feet up on the coffee table. She shut her eyes and imagined Nick coming back on his knees to apologise and beg her forgiveness. She'd probably let him in, but she'd be hanged if she'd forgive him. She was through with men.

But, of course, men were not through with Kathryn. Later that day Northrop called, ostensibly to ask about her health, but she could tell that he was curious to hear whether Nick had come to see her.

Kathryn's first impulse was to tell him exactly what she thought of his meddling, but then she decided to give him the same treatment she was giving Julia. Instead of ranting and raving, she played dumb. No matter what leading questions he asked, she pretended not to know what he was talking about.

He was finally reduced to asking if she'd seen Nick and she said, 'Nick? Should I have seen him?'

'Then he hasn't been here?'

'Why, did he say he was coming over here?'

'Well, no, but I thought . . . Never mind. I must have got my messages confused, you know how it is.'

'Yes, I know,' she said sweetly as he rang off. She replaced the receiver and chuckled aloud at her cleverness. 'I, Kathryn Gardner Lawrence, warn the whole world. From now on, you'd better watch out,' she sang to her empty living room. 'Meddlers beware!'

She was right about Nick. He realised how wrong he had been and he even apologised—but in a most unsatisfactory manner. It was a week before she heard from him, and then she had no chance to show how smart she was because he didn't call or come over. Instead, he wrote her a letter. It was short and to the point.

Dear Kathryn,

Please accept my apologies for my behaviour last Thursday. Everything I said was inexcusable, and I do not expect you to forgive me. But please know that I am available if you ever need me.

Sincerely,
Nick

'You coward!' Kathryn muttered as she read the note a dozen times. In the week that had passed since she'd thrown him out of her house, she'd begun to wonder if maybe he was gone for good, but this was almost worse. She was surprised at how hurt she was over the letter's formality. She was sure that she wanted nothing more to do with the man, but she wanted it to be *her* decision, not his.

She let a week go by before she decided to answer his letter, and she made sure that her words gave no more hint of emotion than his had. She wrote several versions before she was satisfied.

Dear Nick,

I received your letter and I accept your apology. I understand that you were under a great strain the last time we met. Please do not worry about me. I am fine and can take care of myself and the baby. I do not expect that we will want to see each other again, but if you want to contact Julia, I have no objections.

Sincerely,
Kathryn

She tacked on the last bit about Julia as almost an afterthought, but as she sealed the letter, she was glad that she'd put it in. She and Julia had made their peace days ago, and she knew that Julia missed her outings with Nick. Not for a minute did Kathryn admit to herself that she missed him, too.

She decided to take her morning constitutional by walking to the post office, and she went to the cupboard to get out her light coat. It was October already and there was a slight nip in the air.

The letter had the effect she had hoped for, and she was not surprised when Julia stopped her on the stairs a few days later to tell her that Nick had called. 'He's finally found a flat he likes and he wants me to go with him to look at it,' Julia said tentatively. 'Of course, if you'd rather he didn't come over here, I'd understand.'

Kathryn smiled at Julia's new caution. It was just

possible that the dear old lady had learned a lesson. Kathryn didn't have the heart to give her a hard time. 'Please go right ahead, Julia,' she said. 'Good heavens, the man means nothing to me.'

Her statement brought a look of disbelief to Julia's face, but the older lady did not press her luck. A short time later, Kathryn saw the silver-grey Porsche pull up across the street from the house.

She stood back from the window where Nick couldn't see her, but a chill went along her nerves when she saw him look up towards her. He might be coming to see Julia, but this was Kathryn's house and he knew it. Kathryn did not stop to examine the comfort she felt that he was back in their lives.

The next day, Julia reported that Nick had liked the flat and planned to move in within the week. 'It's a sublet and it's already furnished,' she said forlornly. 'I was hoping I could help him decorate, but the place isn't half bad.'

'Take heart. Maybe in a year you can help him find a new flat that isn't furnished,' Kathryn smiled. 'Meanwhile, I have a few things I have to pick up at Jordan's for the baby's room. Would you like to come along?'

Julia needed no second invitation, and they set off for shopping and then lunch in the town. Both were pleased that Nick would be around for a while, but only one of them admitted it. Kathryn's pride had been wounded more than she realised.

He was visiting Julia the next Saturday morning when Kathryn went out to buy groceries, and when she returned home, laden with her usual brown bags, he came out into the hall. They stared at each other in embarrassment until one of her bags began to slip.

He moved quickly to take both bags from her arms. 'Here, let me take those. You shouldn't be carrying such heavy things.'

'They aren't that heavy,' she protested, but he was already halfway up the stairs.

Kathryn followed slowly and then saw that he was waiting for her to unlock the door. She fumbled with her keys and was reminded of the first day he had arrived. He'd carried her groceries then.

She looked up at him and she could tell that he was remembering, too. 'I wish we could start all over, Katie,' he murmured. 'I was a fool to go off half-cocked the way I did.' He moved as though to touch her, but his arms were filled with the bags.

Kathryn pulled her eyes away from his. 'I guess it showed what you really thought of me, though, didn't it?' She succeeded in unlocking the door and pushed it open to let him precede her into the flat.

He placed the bags on the counter and turned to defend himself. 'Look, would it help if I told you that my reaction had nothing to do with you?'

She leaned against the door and folded her arms across her chest. 'You mean it was some other woman Northrop wanted you to marry?'

He smiled ruefully, 'No, but there was another woman in my life who did the sort of thing I accused you of. Marlene, my ex-wife, used every trick in the book to get her way.'

He hesitated then blurted out, 'I married her because she told me she was pregnant.'

'But she wasn't?'

'No.'

'Oh.' Kathryn looked away from him. That explained a lot, but somehow it still wasn't enough. 'I'm sorry, Nick, that was a rotten thing for her to do to you, but you're right, it has nothing to do with me.'

'Oh, yes it does.' He came towards her and stood in the middle of the room. 'Your dear Northrop called me into his office just the way my father-in-law did twenty years ago—and he said almost the same things.

I thought for a minute that I had gone back in time—or that I was losing my mind. I tell you it was a nightmare. Marlene's father even looked like Davis!'

Kathryn tried not to smile, but she couldn't help it. 'I wish I could have been a fly on the wall.'

'It wasn't funny.'

'Maybe not to you.'

'Then do you think you can forgive me? Can we try to be friends again?' He walked over to her, but he stopped short of touching her.

She looked up at him at the word 'friends' and realised immediately that it was a mistake. His statement seemed completely reasonable on the surface, but the second their eyes met, she knew that something as simple as friendship was not going to happen between them. His words might be mild, but his eyes said that he still wanted her.

Her own reaction to him was so strong, that she couldn't tear her eyes away. Oh, how she wanted him!

She managed to look aside and then she pushed herself away from the door and walked to the kitchen. She had to clear her throat before she could answer him. 'I'm afraid I'm not feeling quite up to any more friendships with men for a while. I've forgiven you—I think—but for now, well, I've had all I can take for now.'

Nick seemed about to argue his case further, but then he stopped himself and, instead, he nodded. 'I guess I really can't blame you. Actually I never meant to say anything. I should thank you for at least letting me apologise.'

He walked to the door with a meek posture that seemed completely foreign to him, and Kathryn found that she was surprised—and maybe disappointed—that he was leaving so easily.

But then he turned back. 'Oh, I almost forgot the one thing I *did* want to ask you—purely on a professional basis. I'm having a small dinner party for a few of my associates next Friday and I need to find a caterer. I would like to have you do it, though I'll understand if you won't.'

'Next Friday? I don't know.' Somehow it was the last thing Kathryn had expected him to ask. 'I suppose I *could* do it,' she said doubtfully. 'I'll have to check my calendar.' She went over to her desk and got out her appointment book.

The date was open, but she stood there looking at the book not at all sure of what she should do. It would be so simple just to say that her calendar was full. But then she chided herself for being a fool. He was a businessman and he was making a business proposition, nothing else. If he wanted to put their relationship on a professional footing, it was for the best and she knew it.

She turned back to him and inclined her head. 'Yes, I can do it that evening, if you like. Do you want to see a menu?'

'No. That beef-mushroom thing you make will be fine. And don't bother with dessert. I like to take care of it myself. Can you deliver it by seven-thirty that evening?'

'Of course.'

'Very good. Oh, here's my new address.' He took a small pad out of his jacket pocket, jotted down a few lines, tore off the top sheet, and handed it to her.

She looked at it and saw that he had moved to a converted warehouse complex on the waterfront where she'd delivered meals before. He'd also written seven-thirty, Friday on the bottom—as though she could possibly forget.

He was still standing in the doorway and so she nodded and said, 'That will be fine. I'll put it on my calendar.'

'Um, very good. Thank you.' He left like a man

afraid to test his good fortune, and Kathryn couldn't help smiling. He must have expected her to refuse out of hand, and she was glad that she hadn't. She was proud of the cool, professional way she had treated the matter.

After all, what did it amount to? She'd deliver the meal to the door the way she always did, and then she'd be gone. There was nothing more to it than that.

She put the groceries away thinking that it was amazing how easy things were if you just acted like an adult.

CHAPTER SEVEN

SHE was at Nick's door by seven-fifteen on Friday night—fifteen minutes early. The traffic had been light, for once, and she found a place to park without driving around the block.

She'd considered changing out of her slacks and sweater to deliver the meal, but there was no point in looking pretty just to play delivery girl. She'd given much too much thought to the evening as it was.

Her resolutions about being adult and professional were all well and good, but the truth was that, during the week, she'd thought about little else than the fact that she'd be seeing Nick again. And now she was as nervous as a cat.

He did not answer the doorbell on the first ring, and she hesitated before ringing it again. She had a fleeting thought that she might get away with leaving the food by the door with a note attached to it, but then she realised that she'd have no way of knowing if he'd received it, and no assurance that she'd get paid.

'Stop being a coward,' she muttered to herself and was about to press the bell again, when Nick opened the door. He had a towel draped around his neck, and all he wore were jeans which were zipped and not buttoned. His hair was dark with water and he was glowering. It did not take a sleuth to realise that she'd got him out of the shower.

The sight of his naked torso made her self-conscious, and she started to babble, 'I'm sorry. I'm early. The traffic was lighter than I expected and I found a place to park . . .' She held out the food as though it were a peace offering.

Nick seemed to be amused at her unease. He grinned at her and said, 'It's OK, Katie, relax. I didn't mean to snarl. I'm just running a bit behind schedule. Please come in. I'll throw on a shirt and be with you in a minute.'

'Wait——' Kathryn had not intended to set foot in the door. But he disappeared before she could hand him the food—and before she could collect her money. She sighed and entered the hall, and in spite of herself, she looked around with interest at his new flat.

The area she could see was carpeted with a dense beige shag, and the hall walls were covered with a glossy brown oriental-patterned wallpaper. Only one lamp illuminated the living room, but it showed up brown velvet couches and what appeared to be a large mural on the far wall. The place had a masculine but comfortable aura about it, and Kathryn could see why Nick had decided to take it.

She was still standing by the door when he came out of the bedroom, tucking a blue polo shirt into his jeans. 'I thought you'd be spreading things out in the kitchen by now,' he said with a questioning smile.

'I don't . . . I leave that up to you,' Kathryn replied uncomfortably. 'All I do is deliver it.'

'You'll at least show me how to warm it up, won't you?' he coaxed. 'Here, let me take your jacket.' Kathryn found herself divested of her coat before she could refuse, and he was leading her into the kitchen.

As they entered, he switched on the lights and she saw that it was a large kitchen for a flat. Her eye immediately caught sight of an appliance on the counter.

'I see you have a microwave,' she said in her best professional manner. 'All you have to do is put everything in there and then serve it in bowls. Or you can put the food in the bowls first and heat it just before you serve it. Now I'd better get out of here so that you can get dressed before your guests arrive.'

She turned towards the door. but he was blocking the way and she sensed that he was not about to move. Her eyes spotted another door at the end of the room and she made for it, guessing that it must lead to the dining area and thence to the living room and the front door. For some reason she felt she had to get out of here.

The door led to the dining area, and she saw that the table was beautifully set—for two. She had almost walked past it before it registered in her brain that there should have been four more places set.

Nick had told her that the dinner was for six people and she had made food for that number. Either he couldn't count, or he was planning a *tête-à-tête* for two.

Nick had followed her from the kitchen, and when he saw her eyeing the table, he looked sheepish and said, 'I see you've found me out. I didn't expect you to come in here so quickly.'

Kathryn tried to appear indifferent. 'I makes no difference to me how many people you feed, but I hope your guest has a healthy appetite—whoever she is. Otherwise you'll be eating leftovers for a week. She slipped past the table and into the living room. She just wanted to get her coat and get out before Nick could see how upset she was that he was entertaining another woman.

But he came after her and leaned against the hallway cupboard. 'Wait. You're not really going to make me eat alone, are you?'

Kathryn stopped her attempt to open the cupboard door and looked up at him. 'Alone? I distinctly saw a table set for two.'

'Yes, two. You and me. I'm sorry that you had to cook the food, but I knew you'd never come over if I simply invited you.'

'Invited me? You mean that story about a business

dinner was a ruse to get me to your apartment? Why that's . . . it's . . . I'd never have come near this place if I'd known.'

'Exactly.' His grin was not at all repentant. 'But now that you're here, we might as well eat, right?'

'Wrong. I don't like being manipulated. You should have tried the direct approach—like that simple invitation.'

'Would you have come?' He looked surprised.

'No, but then I wouldn't have had to prepare a dinner that no one's going to eat, and you wouldn't have had to pay for all that wasted food.'

'So you expect me to pay you?'

'Of course. I came here in good faith, expecting to deliver the food and be gone. I expect to be paid for my efforts. But for now, I'll settle for my coat so I can go home.' She tried once more to open the cupboard door.

But he did not budge. He looked down at her and said slyly, 'What's the matter? Are you afraid to stay?'

Kathryn shut her eyes and shook her head. 'That line's as old as the hills. Now give me my coat or I'll go without it.'

Nick stood away from the door, but he wasn't through yet. 'Look, if you're not afraid of me, why not stay? It won't hurt to share a meal, will it? I'd really like to make it up to you for my rotten behaviour since I got into town.'

'I told you once that I'd forgiven you.'

'Well then, stay and let me show you how civilised I can be.'

Kathryn shook her head and smiled, she'd got her coat as soon as he'd moved away from the door, but she no longer felt that she had to flee him.

'Thanks for trying, Nick, but I don't think it's a good idea, not yet. Maybe if you ask me some other time—and I don't have to cook—we can have dinner together; but not this way and not tonight, OK?' She began to walk to the door.

Nick followed her, but he seemed to have given up trying to persuade her. When she got to the door, he reached past her to open it, and for a moment, she was almost in his arms.

She jumped a little and he leaned down and whispered in her ear, 'Still think you're not afraid of me?'

The door was open and Kathryn's way was clear to make her escape, but suddenly she changed her mind. She realised that she was acting as though she *were* afraid of the man, and it was silly. Good heavens, what could he possibly do to her?

She took a step away from him, but it was not towards the door. Instead, she gave him what she hoped was a cool, calculating look and said, 'OK, Nick. I'll stay, but on one condition. I want you to pay me in advance for the meal. I delivered it in good faith. It's only fair the you keep your end of the deal.'

Her words seemed to come as a complete surprise to Nick—just as she'd intended. They gave her the upper hand—at least for the time being—and it was a good feeling.

He didn't answer immediately, and so she pursued her point. 'Even if I don't stay, I'd like my money. I don't usually work on credit.'

'And I didn't expect you to.' Nick's voice finally caught up with him. He gave her a respectful grin and said, 'Why don't you hang your coat back up while I get my cheque book?'

Kathryn did as he suggested and then watched as he wrote out the cheque. If he expected her to be embarrassed, she made sure that he was disappointed. She took the rectangle of paper from him and folded it neatly in her purse. Then she led the way into the kitchen saying, 'Shall we warm the food?'

He followed at a leisurely pace and murmured,

'Anything you say.'

Kathryn could tell that he'd got back his aplomb and was enjoying himself, but she was not worried. She had the upper hand. All she had to do was hold on to it.

It took only minutes to get each dish steaming hot in the microwave, and then, to Kathryn's surprise, Nick went to the refrigerator and got out an unbaked and obviously homemade pie. 'Did you make that?' she asked, not trying to conceal her surpise.

'Of course. It's Apple Pie *à la* Varganin. My mother taught me.' He slid it handily into the oven.

Kathryn had tried to make apple pie only once in her life. The crust had come out chewy, and the apples had disintegrated into a mushy mess. She'd decided then and there that she'd never make a pastry chef. But she loved apple pie.

She gave him a begrudging smile and said. 'Maybe you're in the wrong business. *If* it's any *good*.'

'You'll just have to wait and see, won't you?' he returned smugly.

'Yes, I will,' Kathryn agreed. She began to carry the dishes into the dining room.

They kept their conversation to general topics while they ate, and Kathryn was reminded of their day in the country not so long ago. Nick was an excellent host when he put himself out to please, and Kathryn found herself relaxing and responding to the convivial atmosphere he created.

He served an excellent red wine that stood up well to the Beef Stroganoff, but Kathryn made sure she limited herself to one glass.

He casually mentioned that he had switched to a bank other than Northrop's, but he didn't say why, and Kathryn didn't ask. Still, she was relieved that he had. The idea that Northrop had discussed her with Nick had bothered her a good deal.

His mention of business made her think to ask how his own was going.

'About the same as usual,' he replied. 'My clients don't really care where I base myself as long as I'm at their service when they need me. I'll still have to spend half my time on the road. As a matter of fact, I was in San José yesterday and I have to go to Houston Monday. I won't be back in Boston for a couple of weeks.'

'I didn't realise you travelled so much,' Kathryn said. She was surprised at how forlorn she felt that he went out of town so often. It wasn't as though she even knew when he was gone, but she hated the thought of his being away.

Nick shrugged. 'It's part of the business, though I *do* get tired of it. You sound as though you know what's it's like. Most people think travel is exciting.'

'I was thinking of it from your ... um, family's point of view.' Kathryn had almost said 'wife's' and she quickly tried to cover her tracks. 'I mean, if you had a family, they'd never see you.'

'Then it's lucky I don't, isn't it?' Nick looked at her as though he suspected that there was more to her words than she intended him to see.

The topic had suddenly become dangerous, and Kathryn didn't know how it had happened. But she *did* know that she'd better lighten the atmosphere—and quickly. She reached for the nearest bowl and asked, 'Would you like some more rice?'

He looked amused at her transparent manoeuvre and shook his head. 'No, thank you, I've already had three helpings of everything, but I'm ready for coffee. Shall we have it in the living room?'

'Yes, that will be fine.' He'd already risen from the table, and she followed him into the kitchen to get the coffee tray.

She wished she could think of some good reason to

leave immediately, but she told herself not to panic. Nick had no idea that he was close to breaching the wall she had erected between them, and all she needed to do was play it cool.

They made the coffee and carried it into the living room. Kathryn sat on a chair rather than the sofa, where he might try to join her, and he gave her a knowing look and sat across from her. 'I sense that you still don't trust me,' he said mildly.

Kathryn took a sip of her coffee and looked at him over the rim of her cup. It was herself she didn't trust, but he didn't know that. Somehow, his mentioning that he was leaving town on Monday had triggered a desire in her for him that she'd thought she'd conquered. It was as though his imminent departure made him suddenly irresistible. In the lamplight his blue polo shirt brought out the blue in his eyes, and the knitted material emphasised the breadth of his chest.

'Hello, are you still there?' Nick got up from his chair and waved a hand in front of her face.

His movement startled her and she almost spilled her coffee. He took it from her and then kneeled down in front of her. 'Hey, are you all right? You seemed to have gone miles away.'

About as far as the bedroom, Kathryn was tempted to say, but she still retained enough sense to control her tongue, if not her thoughts. She gave him an apologetic smile and said, 'I'm sorry, I must be more tired than I thought. I *did* slave over a hot stove all day for this occasion, you know.'

He looked immediately contrite and took her hand. 'What an idiot I am. Of course you're tired. I forgot about your condition.' His eyes went to her waist which was still as slender as ever, but he knew as well as she what it concealed.

Kathryn hadn't thought once of the baby since

she'd arrived, but its father was suddenly looking at her as though he'd just remembered that she was a woman. Their eyes met and Kathryn knew that they were both remembering the intimate moments that they'd shared on the sun-kissed island.

Nick stood up and pulled her slowly to her feet. She came willingly and he leaned down to kiss her gently on the lips. 'I'm glad you came,' he said softly.

She knew he meant his words as a farewell, but their eyes spoke a much more honest language. She put her hands on his chest and lifted her lips for a deeper kiss. His arms slid around her, and his mouth came down to claim greedily what she was offering.

A faint buzzing sound barely penetrated Kathryn's awareness, but she made no connection between it and their inner world. It was like the buzzing of a summer bee.

If Nick heard it, he ignored it, too, until they broke away from each other for a moment to seek the comfort of the couch. Only then, as they pulled slightly out of their trance, did they realise that the sound actually existed and it was coming from the kitchen.

They gave each other a puzzled look, and then Nick hit the side of his head with the palm of his hand. 'My pie!' He groaned and made a quick dash for the kitchen.

Kathryn followed and watched in amusement as he turned off the buzzer and opened the oven door. He had to look through several drawers before he found a pot holder. The pie was deeply browned by not burnt and the delicious smell of apples and cinnamon filled the room.

Nick placed it carefully on the surface and then turned and laughed down at her. 'Do you realise that every time I've tried to make love to you in Boston buzzers and bells have gone off? Do you think it's your Puritan ancestors warning us from the grave?'

'I think it's more likely that we're just a couple of forgetful cooks,' Kathryn said wrly. 'But, still, I think we should heed the warning—from wherever it comes. It's been a lovely evening, but I think I'd better go. I'll have to take a rain check on that pie, if you don't mind.'

'Do you really mean the pie or the kisses?' He was smiling at her as though he knew exactly what was going on in her head.

'The pie, of course, it will be too hot to eat for a while.'

'I imagine we could think up some way to fill the time till it cools, don't you?' He began to move towards her.

Kathryn's common sense shouted, *Get out! Get out while you can!* But something stronger than common sense was taking over her body. She backed away from him, but she made no effort to depart. Instead she said, 'M . . . maybe we could have another cup of coffee?'

'Of course.' He stopped moving towards her and went to hold open the kitchen door.

Kathryn walked back into the living room and picked up her cup which was still full of tepid coffee. But he took it from her fingers and asked, 'Is coffee what you really want?'

Kathryn looked up at him and knew that coffee had nothing to do with what she wanted, and furthermore, she could no longer think of one good reason not to take what they both needed from each other. She was no longer engaged to another man, and Nick was everything she'd ever wanted in a lover. So why shouldn't she assuage the desire that was making it almost impossible for her to see straight?

She gazed up into his eyes and managed to say, 'What I really want is you, Nick.'

She saw only the beginning of his smile as he swept

her into his arms. Their kisses were deep and hungry, and their arms strained to mould every inch of their bodies together.

His hands slid under her sweater, and she pulled his shirt from his jeans to feel the smooth skin of his back and shoulders. When the confinement of their clothing was too much, they broke apart and he suggested, 'Shall we continue in the bedroom?'

He didn't wait for her nod before he picked her up and carried her across the room. With the hand that was under her knees, he flicked on the bedroom light, and Kathryn saw that the room was almost filled by a giant water bed which was covered by a furry brown counterpane. She remembered that the place belonged to a violinist, and she made a mental note to rethink her opinion of musicians.

The trip to the bedroom had given Kathryn a chance to come slightly to her senses, and as Nick carried her into the room, she struggled a bit and said, 'I don't like the look of that bed. I have the feeling it might swallow me whole.'

Nick chuckled and let her slide to the floor. 'I'll take care of you,' he promised.

'That's what I'm afraid of.' Kathryn smiled up at him.

Then her smile turned solemn as she watched him pull his polo shirt over his head and throw it on a chair. 'It's getting warm in here, don't you think?' he suggested.

Kathryn nodded and slowly started to tug her own sweater up and over her head. When she could see again, she noticed that Nick's hand had stopped on the button of his jeans and he was watching her.

Their eyes locked as she reached behind her to unhook her bra, and she was not at all disappointed when his gaze left hers to sweep over her shoulders and breasts. Her skin tingled where his eyes touched her.

They stayed apart for as long as they could stand it, and then the need to close the distance between them became stronger than their pleasure in the delay.

Kathryn felt her breasts crushed against his chest and she ran her hands lovingly over his shoulders and back and waist. Nick pushed her slowly towards the bed and then lowered her to the undulating fur counterpane.

Kathryn had never been on a water bed before, and she was pleased by the way it seemed to gently enfold her body. The fur caressed her skin like a mink coat.

Nick helped her slip off her shoes and the rest of her clothing, and then she watched as he removed his own. She loved the size and strength of his body and welcomed it as he sank on to the padded side of the bed.

He reached over to turn off the lamp on the end table, and their eyes simultaneously caught sight of the telephone. It stood there mute and innocent, but Kathryn's eyes met Nick's and they both smiled.

'I hope you don't have this place rigged to go off whenever the passion level gets too high,' she said, mimicking his words from the last time they'd begun to make love.

'Perhaps we'd better make sure?' he answered, watching her closely.

Kathryn reached over and took the receiver off the hook and then she looked back at him. 'Is that better?' His reply was not in words. He rolled her on to the counterpane and covered her body with his own.

Kathryn had almost forgotten the wonderful weight of him upon her. She wrapped her legs around him and groaned as he sensed her need and entered her immediately. The delaying tactics she'd used had only served to make her desire for him even greater, and she was more than ready for him.

They strained together as though to erase the time

and distance that had come between them, and their passion rose quickly to an uncontrollable level. They climaxed in a wild rocking delirium.

Nick was the only man who had ever released such uninhibited passion in Kathryn, and when they'd been on the island together, she'd been shocked by her response to him. She wasn't shocked now, only full of an expanding, pleasureful relief.

As their breathing quieted down, she found herself smiling. Nick pulled away slightly and smiled back. 'I'd almost forgotten how wonderful you could be,' he said and then lowered his head on to her shoulder.

He began to half-nibble, half-suck at her skin, and she lay quietly beside him and enjoyed the gentle sensation. She knew from past experience that this was just the lull before the real lovemaking began. With the worst of their hunger of each other assuaged, they could take their time to enjoy each other's bodies to the full.

'You know, you're the best tasting woman I've ever known,' he said as his mouth moved from her shoulder, down her arm, to the inside to her elbow.

'I guess that's a compliment,' she said ponderingly, 'unless there were cannibals among your Cossack relatives. You don't have any extraordinary-sized pots in the kitchen, do you?'

'Cossacks like their meat raw,' he growled and proceeded to take a mock bite of her forearm.

'Hmm. They must be easy to cook for, then.' She pretended to consider the matter.

'Until you run out of arms, anyway,' he agreed. He lifted his head and looked over her body for the next tender morsel.

In the dim light from the hallway, she watched him make his decision, although she might have predicted what it would be. His hand moved up her body to cup her small breast, and his head bent to explore what he'd found. His tongue traced her nipple until it rose to a peak to meet the warmth inside his mouth.

Kathryn stroked his hair and felt desire begin to grow again within her. She let him set the pace this time and revelled in the beauty of the feelings he aroused in every part of her body.

He went slowly, letting her subside a little whenever he sensed that she came too close to losing herself. By the time he came into her, her need for him was so great that she received him as deeply as she could and fought to hold him each time he pulled away.

It was a battle that they waged ever more intensely until each cried out, conqueror and conquered, to subside on to the heaving mass of fur and water that was the bed.

Kathryn had not even noticed how the bed had writhed beneath them until she and Nick collapsed together upon it and discovered that it still moved around them. It was a warm cradling motion, and as they relaxed in each other's arms, they were soon lulled to sleep.

They might have slept through the night, but Kathryn awoke with cramp in her leg and, in trying to slide it out from beneath Nick, she woke him up. He pulled her lazily to him and mumbled, 'Are you ready for more?'

Kathryn wasn't sure whether he was serious or still half asleep, but she saw by the glowing digital clock that it was nearing midnight. She had certainly not planned to spend the night, and if she were going to depart, the time to do it was now.

She twisted gently away from him and climbed rather awkwardly off the moving mattress. Her movement awakened Nick more fully and he asked, 'Where are you going?'

'Home,' she whispered, although there was no one

else in the room who might wake up. She groped
around the bed for her clothing and put it on piece by
piece as she found it.

Nick swung his legs over the side of the mattress
and turned on the light. He watched her dress and
said, 'You're welcome to spend the night, you know. I
won't feel compromised in the morning.'

'No, what you'd feel is tired,' she replied as she
slipped on her shoes. 'Didn't you say you had to go to
Houston tomorrow?'

'No. Tomorrow is Saturday. I go to Houston on
Monday. Now will you get back into bed?'

Kathryn had had the impression that he was leaving
immediately, but it made no difference. She knew that
she had to assert her independence in their relationship
from the very start. She had no illusions that it would
last, and she wanted to make it clear to Nick that she
would come and go as she pleased.

'I prefer to sleep in a bed that doesn't slosh around
whenever I move,' she said lightly. 'Don't bother to
get up. I'll see myself out.' She gave a small wave and
walked to the door.

But Nick was already up off the bed and pulling on
his jeans. 'At least let me drive you home. The streets
aren't safe at night.'

Kathryn was halfway across the living room where
they'd left the lights blazing away before she turned
and answered him. 'I appreciate your offer, Nick, but
I came here in my own car, remember?'

Nick followed her to the coat cupboard and helped
her on with her jacket. 'I don't understand why you
can't stay. I won't lay another hand on you if you
don't want me to.'

'That's not it at all and you know it,' Kathryn said
impatiently. She looked around for her carryall and her
bag and realised that she'd left them in the kitchen. She
wanted to leave them, but her keys were in her bag.

She headed for the kitchen and he asked, 'Where are you going?'

'To get my bag.'

They entered the kitchen together, and they both saw the apple pie sitting on the counter. Kathryn found her things as he said, 'Won't you at least stay and have a piece of pie? I made it for you.'

She smiled at his plaintive tone and shook her head. 'I can't, Nick, really.'

'Why in heaven's name not?'

'Well for one thing, Julia usually stays awake until she hears me get home. She's probably ready to call the police by now.'

'Did she know you were coming over here?'

'Yes.'

'Then I don't think she's too worried, do you?'

Kathryn knew that he was referring to Julia's matchmaking attempts, and she had to agree with him. 'No, I guess not. Julia trusts you—I'll never understand why. But I still think I should go home.'

'You haven't come up with a good reason.'

'It's reason enough that I never even planned to stay for dinner, never mind for the night. Until a few hours ago, I didn't even think we could be friends. It's all going too fast for me, and I want to go home. I'll see you in a few weeks when you get back to town—if you feel like calling me—but for tonight, I've had enough.'

Nick stared at her as though she were speaking a foreign language. 'I still don't understand. I thought what happened in there,' he gestured towards the bedroom, 'was pretty wonderful. We could have something good together.'

Kathryn threw her head back and laughed. 'Only a few weeks ago you were accusing me of trying to trap you into marriage. Well, forgive me if I want to make sure that that impression is gone for good. I've learned to value my freedom as much as you do, and tonight I

want to sleep in my own bed.' She picked up her
carryall and strode out of the kitchen into the hall.

Nick followed, but only as far as the middle of the
living room. He seemed to have given up arguing. As
Kathryn opened the door and turned around to say
good night, he looked so unhappy that she took pity
on him and said gently. 'I'll see you when you get
back, OK?'

Nick shrugged and slid his hands into his jeans
pockets. 'Whatever you say. Shall I wait until you call
me?' His voice was forlorn.

'I don't know when you get back——' she began,
but then she caught sight of a suspicious twitching
around his lips and she realised that his meekness was
just a pose.

The grin spread from the corners of his mouth and
soon it took over his whole face. 'I was just checking
to see just how liberated you had become, Katie me
girl,' he chuckled. 'Usually it's the man who leaves the
lady's bed at one o'clock in the morning.'

Kathryn felt her face grow red, but she controlled
the impulse to throw her bag at him. Instead she
smiled as broadly as he and said, 'I don't think I ever
claimed to be a liberated woman—at least not out
loud—but if you want to wait for me to call you,
please do.'

In the air hung the implication that he could wait
forever before she called him, but she didn't say it.
She managed to get herself on the other side of the
door before he had a chance to answer her.

She ran down the stairs and out to her car with the
feeling that she had held her own with him for once.
On the island he'd got the upper hand and he'd kept
it; but in this exchange, she'd proved to be at least his
equal.

But the further she drove away from Nick, the less
sure she became of why she'd felt the need to leave

him in the first place. He might have tricked her into coming to his apartment, but he had certainly not forced her to go to bed with him. She'd been a more than willing partner all the way.

She decided that it had been the unexpectedness of it all that had been too much for her. What she needed was time to think. After all, when the evening had begun, she'd planned to deliver a meal and leave. She hadn't expected to be the main course.

She smiled as she drove the last few blocks home. Nick was full of surprises—most of them decidedly pleasant ones. The trick was going to be to keep her balance with him.

She decided that leaving him tonight had been a good move towards that balance and that she'd be fine as long as she kept her wits about her with him. Holding her own with Nick Varganin was going to be quite a challenge.

CHAPTER EIGHT

AND the first challenge came only a few hours later when she awoke in her own bed and realised that she could have been waking up beside Nick. It had been one thing to leave him the night before, it was quite another to wake up without him. They'd be making love by now if she had stayed.

The thought made her ache with desire and frustration until she grew impatient with herself and threw off the blankets and got up. The sun was streaming into the windows, and she knew that she and Nick would have found something wonderful to do with the day. She called herself all kinds of idiot, took a cool shower, and went down to the kitchen to munch some cereal and try to figure out what to do to take her mind off that dratted man.

Normally she had no trouble filling her days, but this morning all she could think about was what she'd be doing if she were with Nick. When they'd been on the island together, they'd always made love first, and then they'd taken turns making breakfast and serving it to each other in bed. After that they'd gone for long walks along the beach.

Today they might have gone for a drive in the country to see the autumn colours. It was the end of October and perfect Indian summer weather for a walk through the leaves and a picnic outside. She remembered that he had told her on the day they'd driven out to Concord that his father used to take his family out to buy cider. Kathryn knew just the place to get it.

At that thought, she got up from the table and

reached for the telephone to call him; but as she picked up the receiver, she knew that she couldn't do it. He'd be much too pleased to know that she already missed him.

She replaced the receiver and went to clean up her few breakfast dishes. Then, as she rinsed her one bowl, she had an idea. She decided to go downstairs to see if Julia would like to go for a drive with her instead. There was more than one way to spend a beautiful autumn day.

She knocked on Julia's door and heard her neighbour call out, 'Come in Kathryn, the door's unlocked.'

She opened the door and stuck her head in and called back, 'I just came down to see if you'd like to go for a drive.'

Julia popped out from behind the kitchen door and said, 'My goodness, Kathryn. Come in. I certainly feel popular this morning. Yours is the second invitation I've had today. But you'll have to forgive me, I'm on the phone.'

She disappeared back into the kitchen and Kathryn didn't have to wonder for a moment who she was talking to. She knew as certainly as though she could see him on the other end of the line. She entered the front room and heard Julia say in the kitchen, 'Yes, Nick, that was Kathryn at the door. Would you like to speak to her?'

Kathryn swung around towards the kitchen and shook her head wildly as Julia once more came from around the door, but it was too late. Julia held the receiver out to her on its long extension cord and Kathryn reluctantly took it.

'Hello, Nick,' she said resignedly.

'Hi, Katie, I was just wondering if you were as sorry as I was that you weren't in my bed this morning.'

Kathryn gave Julia a quick glance, though she

couldn't have heard, and answered, 'No, I can't say I was.'

Nick chuckled, 'Liar. But it's good to hear your voice. I was afraid that last night was just a dream, but I can tell by the sound of you that it wasn't. Having regrets already?'

'I'm sure I don't know what you mean,' Kathryn replied coolly. She was aware that Julia could not help overhearing and so she asked politely, 'Did you have some reason for wanting to talk to me?'

'My, my, aren't we the distant one today,' Nick said. 'Yes, I have a reason for wanting to speak to you. I just invited Julia to go for a drive with me. I'd planned to take you this morning after we . . . er . . . got up, but since you walked out on me, I decided to ask a more willing woman.'

'And this has something to do with me?'

'I might still let you come along if you're good.'

Kathryn took the receiver away from her ear in absolute disbelief at his nerve. Then she brought it back to her mouth and replied, 'Your generosity is truly amazing, Mr Varganin, and I'd be overjoyed to come, except that I'd hate to deprive Julia of the sole pleasure of your company.'

Julia had been pretending not to listen, but now she chimed in, 'Oh, do come, Kathryn. I'm sure that Nick will be so disappointed if you don't.'

'I heard that and she's right,' Nick said. 'Don't be difficult, darling, after all, what can I do to you in front of Julia?'

Kathryn smiled and had to admit, 'Not a lot. But I really don't want to horn in on your picnic.'

'You know I'd spend all my time with you if you let me,' Nick replied persuasively. 'Come along with us and don't be a spoil sport.'

'Heaven forbid I should be that,' Kathryn said in mock horror, but then she had another thought. 'I'd come but I just remembered the size of the back seat in your car. Not even a pigmy would be comfortable there.'

'I seem to remember that it's had its uses,' Nick chuckled.

If you only knew, Kathryn thought wryly. She'd like to see his face if she told him the result of the night they had 'used' the back seat of his car. Instead she said, 'It's too bad we couldn't take mine.'

'Is there some reason why we can't?'

'Well no, only I thought you'd——'

'Feel that my masculinity was threatened if I wasn't behind the wheel?'

'Something like that,' she admitted.

'I could drive your car if it would make you feel any better.'

Now he was teasing and Kathryn had to laugh. 'No, I'll drive. Shall we come over and pick you up?'

'Actually I have to go into the office for a few minutes this morning, so I might as well drive over there. I can be there in an hour if that's all right with you.'

Kathryn agreed that it was fine and hung up smiling. She saw that Julia was inordinately pleased at the outcome of the conversation, but she was too pleased herself to try to dim the older woman's delight. It was going to be a good day after all.

As Kathryn went upstairs to change, she realised that she *liked* Nick very much, and it was a good feeling. She made a conscious decision to stop fighting him and enjoy being with him for however long it lasted. A relationship such as theirs was too rare to throw away.

He arrived less than an hour later with a covered picnic basket in his car which he insisted he would put into the boot of her Mercedes himself. 'I don't want you to peek,' he declared, when Kathryn tried to look inside.

They drove north out of the city and up into the hilly countryside of southern New Hampshire. It turned out that Julia hadn't taken a drive out of Boston to see the foliage in many years, and she drank in the beautiful views like a child seeing them for the first time.

'When I was a girl we used to take the train into the mountains,' she said. 'Life was more leisurely then. We spent the whole summer at an inn by a lake and sometimes a week in the autumn. And we had such wonderful picnics.'

'Well, we'll just have to see what kind of picnic we can come up with today,' Nick told her.

They drove until they came to a roadside picnic area which afforded them a grand view of the White Mountains, and there Kathryn pulled off the road.

When they got out of the car, they found that the sun was so warm that it felt like summer. They chose a table that was half in sun and half in shade, and Julia and Kathryn watched in great expectation as Nick got out the picnic hamper.

He opened it as though he were a magician opening his bag of tricks and brought out sandwiches, fruit, cheese, cold chicken, a salad, a bottle of white wine, and to top it all off, the apple pie he'd made the evening before. '*Et violà!*' he produced it with flair.

Kathryn and Julia clapped as though he'd worked a miracle, and they all ate until they couldn't force down another bite.

'You're a wonderful man, Nick,' Julia said as they packed up to leave. 'I don't know when I've ever spent a nicer day.'

'Yes, thank you, Nick. I've had a good day, too,' Kathryn said.

'That's all a man can ask—to be appreciated,' Nick replied. He looked more than a little pleased at the compliment.

They were all a little drowsy on the way home, and Kathryn turned on the radio to help keep her awake. It was evening by the time they pulled up outside the house and Julia insisted on going right inside. 'I'm not used to such a full day, and I need to get to bed early,' she said and promptly left them alone in the hall.

Kathryn smiled at Julia's rather obvious attempt to give them the rest of the evening by themselves, and she turned to Nick and said, 'I'd hate to disappoint her, wouldn't you? Will you come upstairs for a cup of coffee?'

'Yes, but only because she expects it,' Nick agreed.

Their smiles were warm and a little bit more as they walked softly up the stairs. Kathryn unlocked the door and searched for the light switch, but Nick stayed her hand and gathered her into his arms to kiss her as though he'd been waiting quite a while for the privilege.

Kathryn found that she was as eager as he for their embrace, and she smiled against his lips.

'What's the smile for?' he asked suspiciously.

'I was wondering if Julia could tell we wanted to be alone.'

'It wouldn't take an Einstein to figure that out,' he said wryly. He shut off any further discussion with a kiss, and Kathryn was content to be silent.

After a while, it was he who pushed her gently away as he asked, 'Do you still plan to make that coffee?'

'If you want some,' Kathryn agreed, surprised.

'Well, actually, I'm hungry again,' he admitted.

Kathryn laughed and reached behind him to turn on the light switch. 'I imagine I have something edible around here, though the pickings are pretty slim when I don't have a catering job.'

Nick snapped his fingers. 'The picnic basket! There's still plenty of food in there plus half an apple pie.'

He went outside to get the hamper while Kathyrn made coffee, and they ate their second picnic of the day in the living room sitting on the floor by the coffee table.

Nick enjoyed eating as he seemed to enjoy everything, and Kathryn was struck by the idea that she couldn't have chosen a better father for her child. He was intelligent, honest, athletic, tall, at least mildly ambitious, and most of all, he was alive as no one else she had ever known.

She sighed contentedly over her apple pie and he looked at her questioningly, 'Was that a good sigh I heard?'

'The best. I've had a wonderful day, Nick.'

'Does that mean it's over?'

'No, I didn' mean it that way.'

'That's good because I wasn't planning to leave,' Nick said lazily. He leaned back against the couch and looked at her through hooded eyes.

Kathryn stared back at him and felt her insides go soft. She'd never met a man who could so quickly turn the tables on her. He seemed so easy-going that she constantly forgot how determined he could be when it suited him. If she weren't mistaken, he'd just declared that he was going to spend the night.

She had a fleeting worry about what Julia might think, but Julia was no prude and she knew it. 'You take an awful lot for granted, Mr Varganin,' she said sternly.

'Hmm, yes I do.' He picked up the coffee table that was still full of their dishes and placed it to the side so that they faced each other across an empty stretch of carpet.

Kathryn got to her knees in preparation to stand, but Nick reached out a hand and pulled her to his side. 'Would you like me to offer to leave?' he asked mildly.

'Would you go if I asked you to?'

'Try me.' His eyes challenged hers.

Kathryn looked at the carpet and muttered, 'No.'

'What's that?' He put his hand to his ear.

Kathryn cleared her throat. 'No. I don't want you to go.'

'I didn't think so. So come here.' He pushed her gently to the floor and rolled so that she lay beneath him on the carpet. 'It will be nice to make love on solid ground for a change,' he murmured and kissed the tip of her nose.

'I rather enjoyed our ocean voyage on your bed last night,' Kathryn said.

'Ah, now the truth comes out. Why is it you only admit such things when I've got a good strong hold on you?'

'Because you've got a good strong hold on me,' she answered simply.

He laughed lightly. 'Oh, I see. That makes everything crystal clear.' He smiled down into her eyes and began to stroke the hair off her forehead. 'You know I won't ever do anything you don't want me to do.'

'Whether I know I want it or not, right?' She let a tinge of sarcasm enter her voice. 'I'd sure like to know what makes you so smart.'

'Maybe I just find it easier to be honest,' he said. 'Would you be offended if I told you that, rather than make love on this exquisite carpet, I'd like us to take a shower together and then make love in your bed? I've never even seen your room.'

'Are you curious?' Kathryn was surprised.

'As curious as hell,' he admitted, unblushingly.

Kathryn had no objections, but she found it more embarrassing to lead him upstairs and show him where she slept than she'd found it the first time she'd undressed in front of him.

She looked around the room and tried to see it through his eyes—the four-poster bed with the worn patchwork quilt Julia had made for her when she was a child, the plain white walls covered with posters from places all over the world she'd visited with her grandmother.

The furniture was solid oak and old-fashioned, and a huge braided rug covered the floor. It was nothing like the modern decor she'd used downstairs, and she had to keep herself from apologising for its plainness.

Nick looked around and seemed delighted at what he saw. 'A four-poster bed, my God!' He wrapped his large hand around the tall post.

'I've always had it,' Kathryn said as though that explained it all.

'I can tell,' he said. 'I suspected that there was a Victorian maiden buried somewhere under your twentieth-century ideas. Now I know where she lives.'

'That's silly,' Kathryn declared hotly. 'If I were a Victorian maiden, I'd never have brought you up here.'

'But you'd have wanted to, wouldn't you?'

Kathryn laughed. 'Don't you wish.' She went over to her old linen chest and got him out a towel. 'Are you interested in seeing whether I have a Victorian bathroom, too, or does your voyeurism stop at four-poster beds?'

'I *dream* about bathtubs with clawed feet,' he said.

'Then I'm afraid you're in for a disappointment. The bathroom was done over in 1955.'

She was much less self-conscious to shower with him than she'd been to show him her room. They'd showered or bathed together often at the beach, and they each knew where to soap and rub to have the best effect. By the time they were through, they were very clean and very ready to seek the delights of Kathryn's bed.

It was the first time Kathryn had ever brought a

man home to spend the night. Until two years ago, her grandmother had slept in the bedroom next to hers, and since then, she hadn't been in love—until Nick.

It seemed strange to have his head on the other pillow. He'd fallen asleep soon after they'd finished making love, but Kathryn lay awake to stare at the ceiling. She couldn't help wondering if she were doing the right thing in letting him get so far into her life.

She loved having the size and weight of him in her bed, but she knew that she might end up paying a heavy price when their affair was over. It was one thing to plan to keep her emotions under control but a very different matter to actually do it.

She sighed and shut her eyes and decided to take things as they came. Nick would be out of town for the next two weeks, and she'd have plenty of time to come to her senses then.

She awoke from an erotic dream the next morning only to discover that it wasn't a dream at all. She was lying on her stomach, and Nick's hands were doing wonderful things to the lower parts of her body. By the time she was fully awake, she was in another kind of daze in which the most natural thing to do was to turn to the man who kneeled above her and open her arms and her body to his embrace.

She felt him slide inside her and then, arms and legs entwined, they rolled to face each other side by side on the bed. They rocked slowly, together and away, until gradually their smooth motions no longer sufficed, and then Nick rose above her to finish in hard thrusts what his gentle hands had begun.

When Kathryn could think again, she opened her eyes and saw that Nick was smiling at her. She had enough energy to reach over and kiss him, and then she curled up against the warmth of his body and fell back to sleep.

The next time she awoke it was to the sound of rain on the roof and Nick's breathing beside her. Careful not to wake him, she raised herself on her elbow and looked towards the window where the rain obscured everything but the grey tone of the day. It was the kind of Sunday morning meant to be spent in bed, reading the paper, having breakfast in bed, and making love as the need arose.

Nick had taken care of the last so thoroughly that Kathryn decided that she could fairly be expected to provide the other two, and so she slid quietly from beneath the covers, threw on a robe, and tiptoed down the stairs to see what she could find for breakfast.

She started the coffee brewing and then went down to the front door to pick up the paper which was delivered through a slot in the door. Then she rummaged around in the refrigerator until she found the makings for a herb and cheese omlette. She rarely made breakfasts on Sunday or any other day, but this morning she felt unusually domestic. Cold cereal just wouldn't do.

When she went back upstairs with the newspaper under her arm and a tray in her hands, she expected to find Nick still asleep, but he was sitting up with his pillow propped against the headboard. 'The smell of that coffee has been driving me crazy,' he complained.

Kathryn balanced the tray on the rail of the bed and smiled wryly at him. 'I don't recall chaining you to the bed.'

'That sounds like something we can try later,' he grinned. 'Actually I stayed up here because I didn't want to spoil your surprise.'

'Very considerate of you, I'm sure.' Kathryn held the tray with one hand and threw the newspaper at him with the other.

He caught the paper before it could separate in a thousand sections and suggested, 'What if I promise to do all the cooking from now on when we're at my place and you can do it when we're here? Does that sound fair?'

He was making a statement of his future intentions and they were both aware of it. She handed him the tray as she climbed on to her side of the bed and decided not to give in quite so easily. 'What happens if we spend more time at one person's place than the other's?'

'We could always call in a caterer.'

Kathryn wanted to answer his suggestion with a cold glass of orange juice in the face, but she remembered in time that they were sitting on *her* sheets. She controlled herself—at least until after they had eaten—and then it was every man for himself. She didn't mind at all when she ended up with her shoulders to the mattress.

Later, they read the paper and finally got up and showered and dressed. It was the same kind of day they'd had when they'd been on the island together; and when he left that evening to go home and pack for his trip, the house felt doubly lonely for his absence. The two weeks he'd be away seemed like forever.

During the next few days, she felt her life slip back to normal. The weekend receded into the back of her mind as she became busy catering one and sometimes two meals an evening. She enjoyed being busy, but the work begun to tire her, and she made a conscious decision to cut back to a maximum of five jobs a week. Even an entrepreneur needed time off.

She considered renewing some of the friendships she'd let slide while she'd been engaged to Northrop and seeing his friends, but she decided that the time was not right. She was not ready to make explanations to anyone.

The one thing she *had* to do soon was call her

mother in Phoenix and tell her about the baby, but even that, she was not ready to do yet. It was as though she had decided to put her whole life on 'hold' and enjoy the present for as long as she could.

Soon enough the reality of having a baby on her own would catch up to her, and then it would be time to rally friends and family around her. For the time being, she wanted only Nick for as long as the pretty bubble they created together lasted.

And Nick seemed to feel the same way. His two-week trip somehow got shortened to one, and he called Kathryn as soon as he got in from the airport. She didn't hesitate for a moment when he asked, 'Your place of mine?'

'It's your turn to cook breakfast, I believe,' she said.

They spent another wonderful weekend together, and this time Kathryn made no attempt to assert her independence. She got used to the rocking of his water bed, and they even managed to balance on its surface the Sunday breakfast Nick prepared with all the aplomb of a French chef.

Kathryn tasted the crip bacon and bit into a fresh hot roll and declared, 'I should hire you. I could expand my services to include Sunday brunch.'

'I think I prefer to keep our Sundays non-commercial,' Nick replied as he bent over and licked a spot of jam from the corner of Kathryn's mouth.

Kathryn couldn't argue, and indeed, she didn't want to. Her mouth was too full of food, and her heart too full of laughter to change any part of the way things were.

CHAPTER NINE

THE early days of November went by in a blur. Possibly because she intended to make no permanent claim on Nick, Kathryn felt free to call him whenever she wanted to hear his voice, and see him every night. The Katie that Nick loved came to the surface and stayed there.

Kathryn had never before lived entirely for the present, but she lived there now. The future was something she and Nick never discussed. She tried not to even think about it.

Nick took frequent business trips, but he was rarely gone for more than a day or two, and he always called Kathryn as soon as he got home. If their urgency to be together was caused by their knowledge that they would soon part, they did not say it out loud.

They were lying in bed together in Nick's flat when the subject of Thanksgiving came up. It was only a week away but neither had mentioned the coming day. Kathryn was almost asleep in the curve of Nick's body, when he said quietly, 'Kate, I've been meaning to ask what your plans are for next weekend.'

'Next weekend?' Kathryn was groggy and didn't immediately make the connection to the holiday.

'Yes, Thanksgiving, remember? Are you going to your mother's?'

'My mother's?' He had her attention now. She rolled over to face him and said, 'No, I won't be going to Phoenix. It's too long a trip for just a few days.' And she still hadn't told her mother about the baby.

'Then what will you do?' He sounded uncomfortable.

Kathryn had assumed she'd be spending the day with Nick, but she could tell that he must have other plans. 'I usually have dinner with Julia, and I guess I can do the same thing this year. Are you trying to tell me that you'll be going to Connecticut to see your family?'

'Then you won't mind?' Nick's voice was full of relief.

'I'm only sorry you were worried about it.' Kathryn's fingers wandered to his lips. 'I had planned to make you bake the turkey, but I guess Julia and I will manage.'

She felt his lips smile and then she was gathered into his arms. He made gentle lingering love to her without letting her do a thing; and as her body began to tingle all over from the feather touch of his lips and hands, she decided that it paid to be nice.

Kathryn and Julia spent a quiet Thanksgiving together in Julia's flat. They could have invited other friends to join them, but Kathryn suspected that Julia wanted the chance to speak to her alone, and she was right.

They had finished their dinner and were doing the dishes in the kitchen when Julia brought up the subject of Kathryn's future. 'You'll have to forgive an old woman for prying, but have you decided what you're going to do yet?'

Kathryn was surprised that Julia had got all the way through the meal without asking, and she smiled and shook her head. 'I really haven't looked that far ahead.'

Julia's, 'Humph,' was an understatement of frustration. 'Have you at least told your mother, or are you going to arrive with the baby on her doorstep?'

'I think I'll tell her over Christmas when I go out to see her.' Kathryn made the decision on the spur of the moment. 'It's not the kind of thing to announce over the phone, and I have lots of time before I have to tell anyone.'

'Time will go a lot faster than you think, young lady. You and Nick should sit down and make some concrete plans.'

Kathryn could tell that Julia was about to suggest matrimony and it was time to cut her off. 'Nick and I know what we're doing, Julia,' she said.

She hadn't had the nerve yet to tell Julia that she and Nick would not be getting married at all. Julia assumed that it was only a matter of time until the wedding day, and Kathryn did not have the heart to disillusion her.

But Julia's questioning made Kathryn think; and later that afternoon, when she was drinking her usual cup of tea in her living room, she had an inspiration. *I'll go to my mother's and stay there!*

She knew that soon her pregnancy would soon begin to show, and she and Nick would no longer be able to ignore it. They hadn't discussed it directly since Nick's wild accusations about her attempting to trap him, but she knew that he must think about it sometimes. If she weren't careful, he'd end up asking her to marry him because he felt he had to; and she couldn't allow that.

So she'd go away at Christmastime and not come back until after the baby was born. Her mother would understand. All her mother's friends were so sophisticated they wouldn't think twice about a single woman having a baby. They'd probably think she was divorced and using her maiden name.

It was the perfect solution, and once Kathryn made it, she sighed with relief. It was as though a large weight had been lifted off her shoulders, and she took a sip of her tea and smiled. *The rest of my time with Nick will be a gift*, came her pleased thought.

He surprised her by calling late that evening. 'Hi, Kate, I just got back into town. I hope I didn't wake you up.'

'No, I was still awake,' she answered, 'but I thought you were spending the weekend with your family.'

'I had a change of plans,' he said easily. 'Would you like to be part of them?'

'What do you mean?'

'How about spending the rest of the weekend on Cape Cod? I've rented a room for us right on the beach.'

'When did you do this?'

'About five minutes ago. Will you come?'

'Of course.' Kathryn smiled as she hung up and flew upstairs to pack an overnight bag. It looked like her gift of time with Nick would have an early start.

It was two a.m. when they arrived at the hotel on the beach in Provincetown which was at the tip of the Cape. Nick checked them in and then carried their bags to their room overlooking the ocean.

Kathryn breathed in the chilly salt air and listened to her favourite music—the sound of the crashing waves on the sand. The foam on the waves glowed blue-white in the moonlight.

The door to their room led directly out on to the beach, and Nick came back outside as soon as he'd deposited their bags. 'Are you going to come in, or do you plan to spend the night out there?'

Kathryn gave him an appealing look. 'Could we go for just a short walk along the beach first? It's a beautiful night.'

Nick gave an exaggerated sigh, 'I suppose if I don't come along, you'll want to go alone?'

His sigh made Kathryn feel immediately contrite. He'd been driving most of the day. 'Oh, I'm sorry. I forgot how tired you must be. Please go ahead and go to bed. I'll only walk a little way and come back.'

'I wasn't exactly thinking of going to bed alone,' he returned wryly, 'but I'll understand if you find the beach more attractive than me.'

Kathryn laughed up at him incredulously. 'You've been driving all day, and it's two in the morning, and you still want to make love? I'll be here in the morning, you know.'

'And so will the beach.' Before she could argue further, he put a 'do not disturb' sign on the door and propelled her into their room. It had only been twenty-four hours since they'd last made love, and Kathryn was surprised by his urgency. But soon she was caught up in the fever of his desire.

Their jackets and shoes and clothes became a pile on the floor. Kathryn began to walk to the bed, but Nick held her back. He looked at her body and then pulled her hungrily back into his arms.

Kathryn's excitement rose, but still she was not ready when his hands lifted her up and pulled her legs around his waist so that they joined together even as they stood. She opened her eyes in surprise and saw that his face was filled with an almost painful intensity. She felt herself ride with him to new heights of passion and was only half aware when they fell on to the bed with their bodies still entwined.

It was in a daze that they climbed under the covers together and slept as deeply as they'd made love. Nick held her to him as he slept, and it was his confining embrace that woke Kathryn while it was still night.

She gently lifted the arm that lay heavily over her body and looked down at his face in the moonlight which came from the window whose curtains they'd forgotten to close. He looked like a man with a problem which he wrestled with even in his sleep. She hoped that the problem wasn't her.

She got up and shut the curtain against the coming

morning light, and then tried to go back to sleep. If
Nick wanted to tell her what he was thinking, she'd
know soon enough.

But when they awoke together much later in the
morning, Nick's mood showed none of the intensity of
the night before. He pointed to their clothing which
still lay in a heap on the floor and said, 'It looks like
somebody was in a hurry last night.'

Kathryn laughed and arched a brow at him. 'I can't
imagine who it might have been.'

'As I recall, all *I* wanted to do was walk along the
beach,' he teased. 'Do you think I can drag you out
there now?'

He didn't have to ask twice. They took a long walk
in the brisk salty air, came back and had a late
breakfast, and then made love again in their room.
The weekend was like a second honeymoon. It was as
though they both felt the urgency to make the most of
the little time they had left together.

Several times Kathryn was tempted to tell him
about her decision to go and live with her mother until
the baby was born, but she couldn't make herself
break the spell of their perfect holiday.

Sunday evening came much too soon, and it was in the
dimness of the car heading back to Boston that Nick
finally broached the subject that Kathryn knew had
been bothering him all weekend.

They had been driving in silence for almost an hour
when Nick said quietly, 'I've told you something
about my family, haven't I?'

'I know that you have two older sisters who used to
hog the window seats when you went for drives in the
country,' she answered lightly.

Nick smiled and nodded. 'Yes, I have two sisters
and they're both long married with daughters of their
own who are almost grown up now. One of my nieces

had an engagement ring on her finger when she showed up for Thanksgiving dinner.'

Kathryn settled back into her seat. 'My goodness, Nick, are you feeling old? You're only thirty-eight.'

Nick shook his head. 'It's not me, but my father. He'll be seventy next year.'

'Is he ill?' Kathryn asked quickly.

'No. Just getting old enough so that he thinks he can get away with saying anything that enters his head.'

'I take it you didn't like what got into his head.'

'You could say that.' He gave a short laugh and looked at her rather warily before continuing. 'He told me in no uncertain terms that it was time I stopped travelling all over the country and settled down before it was too late.'

'Too late for what?' Kathryn was becoming uneasy.

'What do you think? Too late to get married and start a family. He wants a grandson and he's tired of waiting.'

'You didn't tell him about me, did you?' she asked.

'Are you kidding? He would have thrown me out of the house.'

Kathryn had no idea what to say. She had feared all along that Nick might accuse her again of trying to trap him, but she had no idea that he was under pressure from another quarter. Marriage under such circumstances would be a disaster.

'It sounds to me as though we both had an interesting Thanksgiving,' she said carefully. 'Julia was less than subtle in her suggestions about our affairs.'

'Julia means well.'

'And so does your father, I'm sure, but neither of them has the right to interfere in our lives. We just have to make them see things our way.'

'You make that sound easy,' Nick said, 'but you
didn't see the poor woman my sister invited to dinner.
They did everything but serve her up with the turkey.'

Kathryn shut her eyes as a stab of jealousy went
through her at the thought of Nick being matched up
with any other woman. But then her fellow-feeling for
the other woman won out. 'The poor thing. It must
have been dreadful for her.'

'Whose side are you on, anyway?' Nick gave her a
wounded look.

'It's not a matter of sides but of common decency,'
Kathryn declared. 'If you knew how awful such a
situation is to a woman, you wouldn't have to ask.'

Nick grinned and glanced over at her. 'You sound as
though you'd been there.'

'You don't stay single to my age and get away
unscathed.'

Nick chuckled and said, 'I guess we all have our
own crosses to bear. I'll just have to get used to having
a new "friend" invited to dinner every time I go
home.'

'I suspect you'll survive,' Kathryn said less than
sympathetically. She hated to admit it, but she had
thought that Nick was leading up to a marriage
proposal. And even though she would have refused,
she was still irritated that the idea of marrying her
seemed not to have occurred to him.

She shook her head at her own pervesity and said,
'It's really strange, but we're never satisfied, are we?
We should learn to settle for what we have.'

'Tell my father that.'

'No, it's bad enough that I have Julia to contend
with. I'll leave your father to you.'

'Thanks a lot.' Nick made a face, but then he
grinned. 'You know, you're good for me. I never
thought I'd be laughing at my family's unholy
plotting, but you make me almost look forward to

seeing what happens at Christmas—just so I can come back and tell you.'

Christmas. Kathryn was going to be in Phoenix at Christmastime—and thereafter. She smiled at Nick but didn't tell him her plans. He'd find out soon enough.

December was a busy month. As the days advanced, Kathryn received more and more requests for her catering service, and she was hard-pressed not to promise to do more than the five jobs a week she had cut herself down to. She finally sent out a notice to all her past customers that she was booked through the holidays and would be unavailable indefinitely after that. She knew that it might be hard to re-establish her contacts once she returned home, but she wasn't sure of what she'd be able to do after she had the baby.

She and Nick continued to spend most of their free time together, and one evening he asked her to go Christmas shopping with him to pick out gifts for the women in his family. 'I never know what to get them and usually I end up in the clutches of an assistant in a perfume department or a sweetshop.'

'Perfume and chocolates aren't so bad,' Kathryn protested. 'How can I pick out presents for people I've never met?'

'Just choose things that women like,' he suggested.

'If it were that easy, *you* could do it,' Kathryn laughed. 'Can you at least tell me something about them?'

'Well, let's see.' He scratched his chin. 'Martha is the elder. She used to babysit for me, and I'd sneak out of my room and watch her make out with her boyfriend on the couch. Does that help?'

'Not a lot.' Kathryn gave him a quelling look.

'Well, she liked to read. Is that better?'

'Some,' Kathryn admitted.

He went on to describe the rest of the women in his family, and Kathryn began to see why he knew so well how to please a woman. He had been surrounded by them while he'd been growing up.

She could also see why his father was impatient to have a grandson. His attitude might be old-fashioned; but then, at seventy, he had the right to be as old-fashioned as he liked. She thought of asking Nick more about him, but she decided to let sleeping dogs lie.

Nick said nothing about exchanging gifts with Kathryn, but she bought him one anyway. She found a beautiful blue cashmere sweater that would match the blue in his eyes. She looked through his cupboard one evening to find out what size he wore, and she was surprised to see that he didn't have a lot of clothes other than his business suits. She guessed that he didn't have the patience for choosing clothes and hoped he'd appreciate something new.

She helped him with his Christmas shopping, and kept putting off the day she'd tell him that she was not coming back when she went to Phoenix. She had no idea how he'd react to her plans—possibly with relief? And so she kept her own counsel.

Then one evening a week before Christmas, she learned that he was making plans of his own, and they were nothing at all like hers. He invited her to a dinner that he prepared for her himself in exchange for her help in wrapping the presents they'd bought for his family. He was a good cook but he was primitive in his wrapping ability.

After they'd eaten, they took their coffee into the living room where wrapping paper and gifts seemed to be distributed with equal randomness all over the room. They had to clear themselves a place to sit down.

'You should have had these wrapped in the shops,' Kathryn said as she looked at the chaos around them.

'I never think of it in time,' he explained. 'And, besides, it seems like cheating not to do it myself.'

'But it's OK for me to do it?'

'That's different.'

'Because you made me a meal?'

'Something like that,' Nick agreed. He rubbed his chin and gave her a considering look. 'I've been wanting to talk to you about something, and maybe now is a good time to do it.'

The serious tone of his voice made Kathryn uneasy. She'd felt that something was coming all through dinner, but now she tried to head him off. 'I don't think I can wrap and talk at the same time,' she said quickly and reached for some bright red paper.

But he was not so easily deflected. 'I just want you to listen and hear me through. Do you think you can do that?'

'He wants promises yet.' Kathryn picked up a package and looked around for the tape and the scissors. 'Is what you have to say so boring that I might go to sleep?'

'I don't think so.' His lips smiled, but his eyes remained serious.

Kathryn let her glance meet his for only a second. Then she looked down and pretended a deep interest in her wrapping. *I'm not ready for this, whatever it is*, she thought unhappily.

But her obvious discomfort did not stop him. He began to pace the room, and his first words were clearly meant to shock her. 'I've been doing a lot of thinking since Thanksgiving, and I've decided that we've been wrong trying to act as though there's nothing between us but good sex.'

He paused as though expecting a protest from her, but she kept her eyes on her work and did not rise to his bait. Once before she'd thought he was leading up to a proposal, and she'd been wrong. She hoped she was wrong now. Why ruin these last few days before Christmas—their last few days together at all—with futile discussion?

She heard him clear his throat to fill the rather awkward silence that followed his statement. But then, as soon as it was apparent that she wasn't going to answer, he went on, 'I haven't mentioned the um ... child you're carrying, partly because of the way I made an ass out of myself when I first learned about it, and partly because I had nothing constructive to say. But I've been thinking—especially since I saw my father in November—and I've decided that it's about time we sat down and discussed the problem seriously.'

That got to her. She looked up at him. 'Problem?'

He nodded, not seeing the sudden gleam in her eye. 'Yes. The way I see it, we have several possible solutions. The first thing I should mention is that I'd be completely willing to take the child——'

'Take the child!' Kathryn stood up, clutching the paper and package in front of her. She'd actually started to feel some amusement over his pedantic manner, but he'd fooled her again. Not in her wildest imagination had she considered the possibility. 'You can stop right there. You're way off base with that one. This child is *mine*!'

He smiled put out a calming hand. 'Now don't get all upset. I just wanted to make sure you were listening. I'm not suggesting it as an alternative, only a possibility. Now will you hear me out?'

Kathryn gave him a withering look. 'Do I have much choice?' He had her attention now, and he knew it.

'No.'

'I didn't think so.' She sat back down, and resumed the motions of wrapping.

He resumed his pacing. 'OK, where was I? Oh, yes,

the second possibility. I, of course, could provide support for you until the child is grown. I promise you I would be generous.'

He paused again, and by now, Kathryn realised that this was another one of his prepared speeches, rehearsed in advance and heading for some conclusion he'd be bound and determined to reach no matter what she said. She didn't need child support and he knew it.

She didn't bother to remark upon his suggestion but said instead, 'I assume there is a third possibility coming along next? I can hardly wait to hear what it is.'

Her levity seemed to disconcert him and he hemmed and hawed for a few seconds before he said, 'The third possibility is . . . well . . . it's that we . . . um . . . could get married, of course, what else?'

There it was. She'd known it was coming, but she still wasn't ready for it. Especially when it was said in such a reluctant manner. She decided to take refuge in sarcasm.

She stood up slowly and looked up at him. 'Married! I couldn't possibly be hearing right. I thought you didn't believe in the institution—or was it some other Nick Varganin who said that?'

Nick turned away from her and walked towards the darkened windows. 'No, you're right, and my views haven't changed. But *circumstances* have, wouldn't you agree?' He looked over his shoulder at her.

'Circumstances?'

He started to look uncomfortable. 'This *is* a special case, after all.'

'Special case!' Kathryn shook her head. 'Am I supposed to be honoured or something? You should hear yourself, Nick. You sound like a lawyer.'

'Yes, well, I wanted this to be a calm orderly discussion.' He began to walk towards her.

She backed away. 'You make it sound like some sort of a business deal.'

'Well, can't it be—in a way?'

Kathryn stopped and stared at him. 'You really mean that, don't you? It makes me very glad that I already know what I'm going to do.'

Now it was Nick's turn to look surprised. 'Oh, do you?'

'Of course. I haven't been able to ignore my "condition" so easily as you, and I've made my plans accordingly. I've enjoyed my time with you, but I never expected it to last.'

'You didn't?'

'No, did you?'

He flushed and Kathryn took advantage of his embarrassment to drive her point home. 'I thought I made myself clear before, but I'll say it again. This is *my* child and no one else's. I don't need or want support from you or anyone. What I plan to do—to make it easier for myself and you—is to go to Phoenix to stay with my mother until after the baby is born. By the time I come back, everyone will be so thrilled to see my baby, they'll forget to wonder how I got him.'

'And you think it will be easy after that?'

'I don't think it will be too hard. After all, I'll have the one thing I want the most in the world—a child.'

'People will still wonder who the father is.'

'Let them wonder.'

'That's easy for you to say, but what about *me*? I *know* I'm the father.'

'Do you now? Can you be sure of that?'

'Are you saying I'm not?'

'I'm just saying that it's my own business. I *was* engaged to someone else at the time, you know?'

'Don't try to tell me that you ever went to bed with Davis—I know better——' He stopped as though he realised he'd gone too far.

Kathryn stared at him for a long moment while her amusement over the situation quickly turned sour. 'You *know* better? How can you *know* better? What did you two gentlemen do, get together and compare notes? My god! It must have been quite a scene. Were you both trying to deny paternity?'

'It wasn't like that——'

'I just bet it wasn't. Too bad I wasn't there. I could have saved you a lot of trouble. Did it ever occur to you that it might be neither of you?'

Nick gave an impatient shake of the head. 'Would you please calm down? It wasn't like that and you know it. I've accepted paternity and I'm willing to take the responsibility.'

'How noble of you! Now if you could just get it through your thick skull that I don't want or need you to take that responsibility, we'll be all set.'

'Yours is the thick skull if you think you don't need me.' Nick came towards her, and they faced each other like prize fighters. 'I'm offering to help you, and you'd be smart to accept me.'

'Smart! Crazy would be more like it.' Kathryn threw up her hands and stalked over to the coat cupboard. 'You can save your three-point system for your clients, I'm not buying any, thank you.' She grabbed her coat and stormed to the door.

'Wait!' Nick blocked her exit. 'I didn't mean to offend you. I just wanted you to know your options—I don't plan to force anything on you.'

Kathryn laughed. 'That's good because, in your little list of options, you forgot to mention one—and it's none of the above. I never asked anything of you before, Nick, and I'm not asking anything now except, will you please get away from the door?'

Nick stood aside, but he wasn't quite finished. 'Can't I at least drive you home? We came in my car, remember?'

'I'll get a taxi at Quincy Market. I feel like getting some fresh air.' Kathryn opened the door and went out before he could try to stop her again. She ran down the stairs and out into the street.

CHAPTER TEN

As soon as she reached the pavement, she took a deep breath of the cold December air, and then started walking towards the nearby Quincy Market, which was a remodelled section of the old waterfront and now housed a large variety of shops and restaurants. It was not very late, and the market was full of Christmas shoppers.

Kathryn felt like an Alice in Wonderland who has suddenly popped up into the real world. The scene with Nick had been completely unexpected. She couldn't believe that only a few weeks ago she'd actually been disappointed because he *hadn't* proposed.

He'd listed her options as though she were buying a new car. As though she'd be impressed by his *thoroughness*. Men and their orderly minds!

And then to have him throw Northrop in her face and admit that the two of them had discussed her! It was way beyond the limit.

Kathryn blew out her breath and watched it stream into the cold night air. Out of the corner of her eye, she thought she saw Nick, but when she turned her head he was nowhere in sight. Still, she felt as though she were being followed, and she wished suddenly that she could leave Boston immediately and never see Nick again. The whole city could drop into the ocean for all she cared.

She hailed a taxi, and as she rode home, she considered calling the airlines to try to move up her departure date, but she finally decided against it. There were only five more days to go before she left, and in that time, she had to shut up her flat and see Julia off for Palm Beach where the elderly lady spent every Christmas with friends. Surely she could handle Nick for five short days—assuming he even tried to see her again.

When she got home, she made herself a cup of hot chocolate and got ready for bed. She expected to sleep poorly that night, and she did—but for a reason she would never have expected. As she lay there trying to relax enough to sleep, she felt a funny tickling sensation beneath her stomach. It took her a few minutes to realise what it was. The baby was moving inside her.

She caught her breath and put her hand to her stomach, but she couldn't feel it from the outside. It was just the tiniest fluttery sensation, as though the baby were tickling her in the womb.

She smiled in wonder and then felt herself sober. It was the most glorious sensation in the world, but also the most scary. This baby was soon going to become a child she'd have to take care of.

She thought immediately of Nick, and how much he would have appreciated being with her at this moment, and then suddenly she had a terrible thought. What if it wasn't the mother Nick wanted but the child? As soon as the idea came to her, she knew it was a possibility.

She'd been so upset over his awkward marriage proposal that she hadn't been listening to what he said, but she remembered now that his first choice had been to take the baby and raise it himself. In his little list of 'options' that had been the first choice. How could she have missed it?

'Not on your life, Nick Varganin!' she swore. She put her hand on her stomach in a protective gesture, but she did not feel the fluttery sensation again that night.

*   *   *

Late the next morning a delivery boy arrived with two dozen long-stemmed roses. Julia came out of her flat when the doorbell rang and was thrilled at the sight of the long box.

But Kathryn was not so ready to jump for joy. She had too many reservations now about anything he did. The card read simply, 'I'm sorry. Love, Nick.'

Julia peered around Kathryn's elbow and she tsk tsked as she read the card. 'Lover's quarrel?'

Kathryn turned with the box in her arms and held it out. 'It's something like that, Julia. Would you like to have these?'

'Oh, no. I couldn't take them. They're for you.' But then she hesitated, 'Well, maybe just a few. I'll be leaving in two days, but it will be nice to have them until then.' She lifted a few buds and sniffed them appreciatively.

Kathryn followed Julia back to her apartment and decided that it was as good a time as any to tell her old friend about her real plans. Julia would be hurt to come back from Palm Beach only to learn that Kathryn was staying in Phoenix.

As she separated some of the flowers on to the kitchen surface, she remembered how well Julia had accepted the news about the baby, and she hoped for as good a reaction this time.

'I think you should know, Julia,' she said firmly, 'I don't plan to see Nick again. When I go to my mother's, I'm going to stay there until after I have the baby.'

'My goodness, that must have been some quarrel you had last night.' Julia was reaching for a vase and she looked at Kathryn over her arm.

Kathryn shook her head. 'This is no spur-of-the-moment decision. I realise that you expected Nick and me to get married and live happily ever after, but you should know by now that my life doesn't work that

way. I don't trust Nick not to——' she almost said,
'Try to steal my baby,' but that sounded so
melodramatic that she changed it to, 'I don't trust him
not to run out on me just the way my father did.'

'If you ask me, you're the one who's running out,'
Julia said tartly. 'You haven't given the man a chance.
Come to think of it, when has a man *ever* really had a
chance with you?'

'That's not fair. Besides, this is not my future but
my baby's I'm talking about. I know what I'm
doing.'

'You *think* you know what you're doing,' Julia
muttered. 'I suppose these flowers from Nick are a
goodbye present?'

Kathryn hadn't thought of them that way, but she
supposed they could be. 'I'm sorry,' could mean that
he was merely sorry that they had quarrelled, or it
could be goodbye.

'I don't know what they mean, Julia, but I hope you
enjoy them,' she said. 'I'm going to put mine in water
before they wilt.' She took the rest of the roses and left
Julia's flat before they could end up arguing about
things that were already decided.

But as she put her own flowers in a vase, she
couldn't help wondering if they might indeed be the
last she heard of Nick. Would he give up the baby so
easily? Somehow she doubted it.

She put the roses by the window and then kept
herself busy for the rest of the day by writing out the
Christmas cards she'd been putting off sending.
Normally she wrote a newsy little note in each card,
but this year her news was not exactly the Christmas-
card variety. She compromised by telling everyone
that she'd write to them in the new year.

The next day she catered the last meal she'd
scheduled before her departure, and she was sorry that
she hadn't scheduled a few more. It was the eve of

Julia's trip to Florida, but her own departure was still three days off.

When she came back from delivering the meal, she stopped by her neighbour's flat to find out what time Julia wanted to leave for the airport the next morning, but Julia had a surprise for her.

'I should have told you, my dear. Nick is taking me to the airport. Since you and I are both going away, I've asked him to keep an eye on the place while we're gone. I hope you don't mind.'

Kathryn sighed. She might have expected a last-ditch effort on Julia's part to bring Nick back into the picture. 'I wish you hadn't, Julia. You know I always take care of such things myself.'

'Well, it won't hurt to be double safe, now will it?'

'No, I suppose it won't.' She smiled and kissed Julia's wrinkled cheek. 'I know you mean well, you old busybody, but it's not going to make any difference at all. Now take care of yourself and have a good Christmas. I'll write to you as soon as I settle in, OK?'

Julia's eyes became teary and she had to sniff before she could answer. 'You always were a stubborn child who had to learn things the hard way. You're wrong about Nick, but you'll never listen to me. You just remember that if you ever need me, I'll always be here, understand?' She took out the lace handkerchief she kept in her cuff and blew her nose.

Kathryn's own eyes had filled with moisture as Julia spoke and she sniffed and said, 'I know very well that as soon as I come back you'll be giving me as hard a time as ever, you old fraud. Now take care of yourself and say hello to eveyone in Palm Beach for me.' She hugged Julia again and then fled up the stairs.

She heard Nick arrive to pick up Julia the next morning, and she went to the window to see them drive away. They did not see her. The house was quiet after they'd left, and Kathryn was glad that she had only two more days before her own departure.

She was busy going through her cupboards to find what few clothes she could pack that would fit her until she bought some maternity things in Phoenix when she heard someone come in the downstairs door. Her heart skipped a beat, but then she heard loud and confident footsteps on her stairs and she knew it was no thief. It had to be Nick. Julia had given him the key.

He knocked loudly on her door and called out, 'Katie, it's me, Nick. I want to talk to you.'

She left her packing and walked to the top of the bedroom stairs. She was dressed in her baggy house clothes, and had no intention of letting him in to try any more of his tricks. 'I don't want to see you, Nick,' she called back.

'You don't have much choice because I'm staying here until you let me in.' She thought she heard him settle against the wall.

'I don't have anything to say to you,' she said, clenching her hands into fists.

'You don't have to *say* anything. You can just listen.'

'To more of your lies?' she muttered. 'What can you possibly have to tell me that I haven't heard already?' she demanded.

'You won't know unless you open the door.' She heard him shuffle around as though he were growing impatient.

She came down the stairs and stood facing the door. 'Look, Nick, would you please just go away? I don't need this.'

'I think you do. Now let me in and if you don't like what I say, I'll go away. Fair enough?'

'You'll *promise* to go away?'

'Scout's honour.'

'OK, but you're not going to change my mind.'
Because I'm on to you, she finished silently.

She stood aside as he entered with his overcoat on
his arm. He laid the coat on a chair and then turned
and asked, 'Would it be too much to ask for a cup of
coffee? That airport traffic was brutal.'

He was wearing a white cable-knit sweater over grey
slacks, and Kathryn resisted the impulse to apologise
for her own clothes. He'd seen them before. She
poured the last of her morning pot of coffee into a cup
and handed it to him. 'Did Julia get off all right then?'

'Yes. I saw her on to the plane,' Nick answered.
'Won't you have some coffee with me?' He sat on the
edge of the sofa.

'I've had all I can take this morning,' she said as
she seated herself on a chair opposite him. She hadn't
intended her words to have a double meaning, but his
raised eyebrows told her that he had caught her
hostility.

His eyes scanned the room until he saw the roses in
a vase by the window, and he smiled wryly and said,
'At least you didn't give them *all* away.'

'There were plenty to share.' She realised that he
must have seen the other dozen in Julia's apartment.

'They came with an apology.'

'I *hoped* it was a goodbye.'

'Now is that a nice thing to say?'

Kathryn got to her feet. He was trying to put her on
the defensive, and she wasn't going to let him do it. 'I
don't think there's anything—nice or otherwise—for
us to say. You shouldn't have come.'

'Shouldn't I?'

'What are we playing, twenty questions? Why don't
you tell me why you're here, and then you can go.'

'I'd be glad to if you'd sit down and stop being so
hostile.'

'What did you expect—open arms and a kiss hello?'

'It would have been nice.' His face creased in a smile.

'Fat chance,' Kathryn mumbled, but she felt her face trying to smile in return. *Don't let him get to you*, she gave herself a stern mental command.

'What I'm here for,' Nick began, 'is to apologise again, this time in person, for the way I handled things the other night. I don't think you understood what I was trying to say.'

'And you've come to clear it all up?'

'If I can.'

Kathryn sat back in her chair and looked at him. *She* suspected the true motivation behind his coming, but she wondered if he even admitted it to himself.

He cleared his throat and said, 'I think I confused the issue last time by not making my own desires clear. I wanted to show you that I was flexible, but I didn't tell you what I thought was best.'

'You have a preference, have you?'

He ignored her sarcasm. 'Yes, and if you'd stayed calm the other night, I would have told you.'

'Am I calm enough now?'

'Are you willing to listen?'

'I'm willing to get it over with.'

'That will do.' He was silent as he seemed to be marshalling his thoughts. Then he leaned his elbows on his knees and looked straight at her. 'What I was trying to say the other night was that I want to marry you,' he said. 'We are both adults and we're going to have a child together. It's our responsibility to do the best we can for it, and that means marriage.

'I know how little trust you have in men. You told me about your father, and Julia says you still think about him; but I'm willing to promise that—no matter what happens to us—I will never desert our child. I plan to settle a trust fund on him as soon as he's born.'

'It's *my* child, not *our* child,' Kathryn corrected

him. 'Now let me get this straight. You've talked to Julia about it now? Would you like my mother's telephone number in case I have anything more I'd like to hide?'

'Now that's not fair. Julia just wanted to help me understand you.'

'Understand me? How about understanding yourself? You don't want to marry me. You just want to give your father a grandson. Maybe you should wait and see. Maybe it will turn out to be a girl.'

'And maybe she will turn out to be as ornery as you.' Nick jumped to his feet and grabbed her by the arms.

'Let me go!'

'I'm not letting you go until you start talking sense.'

'Sense! I am the only one here who *is* talking sense. You don't want to marry me, and I don't want to marry you.'

'Oh, don't you? Are you sure of that?' He bent his head towards hers and captured her lips before she realised what he meant to do. His hands pulled her to him, and she felt a shock of response go through her. She knew that he must have felt it, too.

She tore her mouth from his and said, 'This is just physical, Nick.'

'About as physical as you can get,' he agreed. He didn't let her go, but pushed her backwards until the couch hit the back of her legs. Then he let her fall beneath him to the cushions.

She tried to push him off her, but he captured both her arms and pinned them above her head. 'Relax. I won't do anything you won't want me to do.'

'Is this why you came here, to rape me?'

'Let's just say it's a spur-of-the-the-moment inspiration,' he grinned. He bent his head and kissed her neck and throat down to where the cloth of her shirt stopped him. He opened her buttons with his teeth, and she felt her breasts rise to the warmth of his mouth.

As soon as he'd touched her, she'd realised that her desire for him had not lessened one iota, and if he did any more thorough examination of her body, he'd know it soon, too.

'This isn't the way to decide anything,' she said, as he began to trail kisses down her stomach. He didn't answer, but he let her hands go and looked into her eyes as his fingers loosened the drawstring of her trousers.

An involuntary groan came from her throat when his hand slid between her thighs. He bent over again, and instead of pushing him off, she began to help him out of his clothes.

His lovemaking was familiar yet new, as though the rift between them over the past few days had added a certain strangeness to the powerful chemistry between them. Kathryn found herself savouring the taste and feel and smell of him until her senses became one incoherent mass of pleasure. She felt herself let go completely as he entered her and brought their union to a thundering climax.

When it was all over and they were resting together on the cushions of the sofa, she found herself smiling, and her first thoughts were, 'This will be a very good thing to remember.'

Nick raised himself on an elbow and saw her smile. 'I thought this might convince you,' he said. He lowered his head and licked away a drop of perspiration that had settled in her navel.

When he raised his head again, he seemed to be studying her belly; and then he cocked an eyebrow and said, 'It seems we'll be getting married not a minute too soon.' Kathryn knew that he referred to the new mound her stomach made. It brought her back to the reason she could have nothing more to do with him. It was *her* baby, not his.

At that moment she felt a tiny kick inside her, and she had the uncanny feeling that the baby was responding to Nick. She was tempted almost beyond restraint to tell him about it, but she knew that she dared not.

Instead she said gently, 'I'm not going to marry you, Nick.'

Nick looked at her as though he couldn't be hearing right. 'What do you mean?'

'This was very nice.' She touched the skin on his chest. 'But it hasn't solved anything, not really. We've know all along that we're attracted to each other. It makes for a wonderful affair, but we can't build a marriage on it.'

'But what about our child?' He put his hand on her stomach and it was almost her undoing. He *did* care about the child if not enough about her.

But that was no solution, and she held on to that fact for dear life. 'What you propose would really be a kind of marriage of convenience, don't you see?'

'And you'd never settle for that, would you?'

'Of course not——'

'Of course not?' He pushed himself away from her and started pulling on his clothes. 'Of course you'd never marry a man you didn't love,' he said sarcastically. 'Certainly not for the sake of a child! Why were you marrying Northrop? Because you loved his money? You never even went to bed with the man.'

'That was different,' Kathryn tried to explain as she found her own clothes and pulled them around her.

'Different?' Nick stood above her and seemed to loom over her. 'What *I* see is that *he* was good enough for you and I'm not. Is it because I'm not rich enough? Or because my family didn't come over on the *Mayflower*?'

'You don't understand.'

'You're damn right I don't. If you try to tell me you loved him, I'll throttle you.'

'Of course I didn't love him. I *liked* him. I knew exactly who he was and what to expect of him. He was safe and predictable, and I expected to have a safe and predictable life with him.'

'And I've ruined everything for you, have I?'

'No. You've straightened everything out. You've made me see that I should never settle for a marriage that is less than I want it to be—and that means with you, too. I've learned my lesson.'

'And I get credit for teaching the course?'

'You've helped me a lot, Nick.'

'Thanks.' He looked away from her and she knew that he was not going to argue any more. He had finished dressing except for his white sweater, and he pulled that over his head and reached for his coat.

'I only came over here to tell you that I was willing to marry you. I didn't realise that you were looking for a knight in shining armour. Good luck in finding one.' He strode to the door and pulled it open.

'Nick!' she called out in spite of herself. She stretched out her arm and made a supplicating gesture, but all she could think of to say was, 'I'm sorry.'

He gave her a derisive smile and answered, 'So am I.'

He turned to leave and then seemed to change his mind. With his hand on the doorknob, he looked back over his shoulder at her and said, 'You know, in a way it's funny. When I first arrived in town, I was the confirmed bachelor and *you* were the one who was insisting on marriage—oh, not to me, I admit—but you seemed to think it was the solution to all your problems.

'Now look at us. I'm practically begging you to marry me, and you act as though I'm making an indecent proposition. This has got to be one for the books.' He shook his head and then shrugged. 'Take care of yourself, Katie.' He gave her a long look that bespoke his frustration and then he opened the door and was gone.

'Goodbye, Nick,' Kathryn whispered as she listened to his footsteps echo on the stairs. She wanted to run after him and call him back, but she stayed where she was in the centre of the room.

She had never wanted a man so much or been so sure that he was bad for her. There was no possibility that a wild affair like theirs could last, and she couldn't take a chance on giving him a claim to her child.

The thought of the child helped calm her and she put her hand to her stomach and patted it lightly. 'I'll take care of you,' she said soothingly.

As she heard the sound of Nick's car revving up and driving away, she went back up to her bedroom to finish packing.

CHAPTER ELEVEN

SHE had got out two large suitcases for her clothes, but by the time she went through all her things, she found very little that would fit her over the coming months. She put one of the cases away and concentrated on packing the things that she could still wear—shoes, nightgowns, underwear.

By the time she was finished, only half of the suitcase was full. She added most of the presents she'd bought for her mother and George, and the rest fitted in a small shopping bag. The present she'd bought for Nick, she left on a shelf.

The next day, she made the final arrangements for her departure. She gave a set of keys to the agency that would watch the house for her, and she took her car to a local garage to be stored. As usual, the mechanic offered to buy the big old Mercedes, but Kathryn replied, 'You just make sure that when I get back, it has had no more miles put on it than it does now.'

Men should pursue women as diligently as they pursued cars, she thought ruefully. The same mechanic had been trying to buy her car ever since her grandmother had left it to her two years before.

That afternoon it snowed, though only enough to cover the ground, and Kathryn took a walk along the Charles River. She realised that the next time she took this walk, it would be summer again and she'd be pushing a pram everywhere she went. The idea excited her even as she shivered a bit at the thought of the great responsibility it would be.

The next morning she ate the last of the fresh fruit she had in the house, turned off the refrigerator, and checked that all the windows were locked. The last time she'd gone through such a routine, she'd been heading for Europe with her grandmother, but this time she had an adventure of a completely different nature in front of her.

She called a taxi, took a last check around the apartment, and then waited by the window until the taxi pulled up. She'd already caried her suitcase and shopping bag down to the front hall, and so when the cab arrived, she slipped on her coat, locked the door, and ran down the stairs.

She picked up the bag, intending to let the driver carry the suitcase, but when she opened the outside door, she was just in time to see Nick pay the driver off and send him away down the street.

She ran out on to the step and waved her arms and called, 'Wait! Wait!' but the driver either didn't see her or pretended not to.

Meanwhile Nick came up the steps and said, 'Relax. I'll take you to the airport. Where are your suitcases?'

Kathryn stopped waving her arms and turned to stare balefully at him. 'Just what do you think you're doing?'

'Would you believe that I was driving by and decided to offer you a ride?'

'No.'

'I didn't think so.' He shrugged and climbed a step closer to her. 'Why don't we throw your suitcases in the car and I can tell you on the way to the airport?'

'I'd rather call another taxi, thank you.' She pushed up the sleeve of her tan trench coat and looked at her watch.

'Don't be silly.' He came up another step until his eyes were level with her own. His gaze trapped hers and he said persuasively, 'What can it hurt to talk one last time?'

Kathryn suddenly knew by the way she was

drinking in the sight of his clear blue eyes and mocking smile that it could hurt a lot. 'I have nothing more to say to you, Nick.'

'Then you can listen while I get in a few last paragraphs.' His look was ironic, and dared her to admit that she was afraid of him.

She pulled her coat around her and glanced away from him down the street. 'What possible good can it do? I'm not going to change my mind.'

'Then you have nothing to worry about, do you?' He hadn't taken his eyes from her face.

She forced herself to meet his glance. 'No. I don't, so it's not worth your time, is it? I'm going to call another cab.' She turned to go back inside.

'You're afraid I'll make you change your mind, aren't you?' His hand was on her arm.

'The only thing I'm afraid of is that I'll miss my flight.'

'Then get in the car before I get a ticket for double parking.'

Kathryn paused stubbornly with her hand on the doorknob, but he'd boxed her into a corner and he knew it. 'My suitcase is inside the door,' she capitulated haughtily.

He put the case in the boot while she got in on the passenger side of the car, and they both were silent as they drove off in the traffic.

It was only after they'd been driving for several minutes and Nick hadn't said a word that she finally took her gaze from the streets and gave him a sidelong glance. He was calmly driving and seemed in no hurry to speak.

She looked away, but at last the silence got to her and she muttered, 'I thought you wanted to talk.'

'I do.'

'Then what are you waiting for?'

'You.'

'What's that supposed to mean?'

'I'm waiting until I think you're ready to really listen to me.'

'It seems that all I do lately is listen to you. What do you want?'

'I want you to hear me with an open mind for a change.'

'OK, it's open.'

But he didn't answer. She waited but the silence grew long again until she finally broke it. 'OK, if you won't say anything, then I will. In case you're planning to go over the same old ground, maybe we should get something straight—right at the start. I will not, nor do I ever plan to, marry you. You've done your duty and proposed, but neither I nor my child need a man who, deep down, is allergic to marriage.'

'What about a man who is hopelessly in love with you and knows that the rest of his life will be worthless without you?' Nick spoke in a matter-of-fact voice, never taking his eyes off the road.

'That man doesn't exist,' Kathryn denied.

'Are you so sure of that?' He gave her a quick, mocking glance.

'Of course I am. What is this, some new kind of ploy?' Had he realised that his emphasis on the baby had been the wrong strategy?

'If you call the truth a ploy.'

'The *truth* is that we have good sex together. You said it yourself. We don't have love.'

'Don't we?'

'You know we don't.'

'Then do you have lots of "good sex" with men you don't love?'

'We're not talking about me.'

'Then let's talk about you.' He gave her a tight smile. 'Do you hate me? Is that it?'

'No, of course not.'

'Then you like me a little—even a lot?' He was teasing now and trying to make her smile.

But she would not. 'What I feel has absolutely nothing to do with anything,' she cried. 'I know what you're trying to do, Nick, and it won't work. You realise that you won't be able to get your hands on my baby unless you sweet-talk me into marrying you. But you can forget it because I'm on to your tricks.'

'My god! Is that what you've talked yourself into believing now? That I want the baby? What would I do with a baby?'

'Give it to your father for his seventieth birthday.'

'And what would he do with it but give it right back? He can't take care of a baby.'

'That's not what I mean and you know it. You'd probably let me bring him up until he was old enough to go to school and then try to get custody.'

'That's ridiculous!'

'Is it? Lots of men get custody nowadays.'

'But I want *you*, not a baby. You've got to believe that.'

'What I *know* is that you never even thought of marrying me until after you went home and your father gave you a hard time about giving him a grandson. You think you'll get the package all in one and get it over with. You don't care about me. The first thing you offered to do was take the baby and bring it up yourself. What was I supposed to think?'

'That I'm a stupid fool, I guess.' Nick laughed and shook his head. 'I figured you'd never believe it if I suddenly told you I loved you and wanted to marry you, so I decided to use the rational approach. I thought I could reason you into marrying me and then let you find out later how much I loved you. I figured you cared more about the baby than me, and if I showed that I cared about it, too, you'd marry me for the child's sake.'

He laughed again. 'My God, I'd never want the baby without you! I never even considered it. What happened at Thanksgiving was that I found I wanted you there with my family. When they brought along another woman, all I could think of was how much they'd love you. Let me tell you, it shocked me. I thought I'd never want to get married again.'

'You didn't say that when we went out to the Cape.'

'I wasn't ready to believe it then,' he admitted.

'Well, I'm not ready to believe it now, so you can forget it.' Kathryn folded her arms and stared stonily out the window.

'Are you that much afraid of love?' Nick's question seemed to come out of the blue.

'What do you mean by that?'

'I think you know what I mean. Look at yourself. A man has just told you he loves you and wants to marry you and you're stiff as a board.'

'I'm ignoring you.'

'Have you ever asked yourself why?'

'Why what?'

'Why you're afraid of love.'

'Look, Nick, I've had about enough of this.'

'You're just getting nervous because you know I'm close to the truth. I've been doing a lot of thinking about you; and from what Julia said and what you've let slip yourself, I can see a definite pattern.'

Kathryn continued to stare out of the window in hopes that her show of indifference would stop him, but it didn't. 'You've been close to marrying how many times—twice, three times?' he asked.

She didn't answer so he answered himself. 'There was the boy in college, then some Frenchman, and then poor Davis. You found a reason not to marry any of them, didn't you?'

'Now wait a minute. None of that was my fault.'

'Wasn't it? You let your grandmother take you to

Europe the first time, and then the second time you let her call you home from Paris. And with Davis you went away and had an affair with me. Only he was too smart for you, he forgave you, and so you had to find another reason to ditch him.'

'You're crazy.' He was echoing the suspicions that Kathryn had once had about herself, and she didn't want to hear them. 'There was nothing stopping either Jerry or Paul from waiting for me when I had to leave them,' she cried. 'They both found someone else very quickly. And I chose Northrop just becasue he *was* so steady and reliable. I didn't get pregnant on purpose. I never even thought about the possibility.'

'Maybe not consciously,' Nick agreed, 'but who knows what goes on deep in our minds? I'll have to admit that Davis was different, but he still let you go too easily. You have it in your head that men are unreliable and you keep setting up situations to prove it.'

'With a lot of co-operation from the men involved,' Kathryn said sarcastically.

'Exactly. You keep picking men who don't stick when the going gets tough.'

'And I'm supposed to believe that you are the exception to the rule?'

'Right the first time! You may have chosen me because you thought it was a safe bet that I'd never opt for marriage, but this time you were wrong. I'm going to stick like glue. I love you and I want to marry you, and I'll follow you around the world if I have to.'

'But I haven't said that I love you.'

'You can any time now.'

'I tell you what. If you still want me when I come back from Phoenix, I'll consider it.'

'So you think you're going to get away that easily, do you?'

'In about an hour, yes. That's when my plane takes off.'

'Is there nothing I can say that will persuade you to stay?'

'I'm afraid not, Nick. You forget. You told me yourself that you didn't believe in marriage, and on top of that you're divorced. Why should I believe you've changed?'

'Marlene left me. I didn't leave her,' Nick defended himself. 'If she'd come to California with me, we'd probably still be married—even if she wasn't the person I thought I'd married.'

'You see, you can never tell about a person.'

'When I met Marlene I was twenty-two years old! Give me some credit for being a better judge of character by now.'

'It wasn't so very long ago that you weren't so very sure about me,' Kathryn reminded him. 'Or did I dream that you accused me of trying to trap you into marrying me?'

'Are we back to that again?'

'It just illustrates my point.'

'But I knew I was all wet the minute I cooled off. Why would you want my child when you were engaged to another man?'

'Why indeed?' Kathryn agreed.

He looked at her out of the corner of his eye and seemed to deliberate before he asked the next question. 'I hesitate to ask this, at such a precarious moment in our discussion, but there is something I've wanted to know for quite a while now. Just exactly how *did* you get pregnant?'

Kathryn had to laugh at his honestly baffled expression. She sensed that he was trying to change the subject, but the opening he'd given her was too hard to resist.

'It happened the usual way, Nick, or didn't your mother tell you about the birds and the bees?'

'It was my father, actually, but you know what I

mean You told me you were protected.'

'I *was*—at least most of the time.'

'*Most* of the time?'

'Don't try to make it look like I planned it—subconsciously or not. In the first place, I was told by a very good doctor that it would take me at least a year to conceive. And in the second place, *I* wasn't the one who insisted on doing it in the back seat of the car!'

Nick didn't look at her, but a grin began to play about the corners of his mouth until finally he could contain it no longer and it spread from ear to ear. 'My god, you mean our child was conceived in the back seat of the car? You're not kidding?'

'Would I kid about a thing like that?' Kathryn was trying very hard not to join his laughter. 'And it's *my* child, not *our* child.'

Nick did look at her now. 'Oh, come on now, Katie, hasn't anything I've said meant anything to you? Do you really want to face your life alone when we can face it together? We've loved each other from the start, and if we'd had any sense at all we'd be married by now.'

His words had the ring of conviction, and Kathryn suddenly couldn't remember any of her arguments against him. She *did* love him. She'd realised it months ago. But she couldn't marry him . . . could she?

'It won't work, Nick, it just won't.'

'OK, Katie, be stubborn if you want to. We'll see who outlasts whom. You may have run away from all the other men in your life, but you're not running away from me. I have reservations on the eleven a.m. flight for Phoenix. That wouldn't be the one you're taking, would it?'

'You wouldn't come with me!'

'Oh no?'

'But you can't. I've made my plans. I *know* what I'm going to do. You'll ruin everything for me.'

'Do you really mean that? Were you *so* looking forward to living alone?'

'I'll have the baby.'

'*Our* baby. I want it, too.'

Kathryn looked at him bitterly. 'You don't know what you're saying. You talk about my being afraid to get married. Why shouldn't I be? Does anything last? I don't want to get married unless it's for *good*. Till death do us part. No easy outs.'

'I want you to meet my mother.'

'What?'

'If you won't believe me, maybe you'll believe my mother. She'll tell you I'm a good risk.'

'What are you talking about?' Kathryn looked out of the window and suddenly realised that they were no longer heading for the Callahan tunnel, but had turned on to the Southeast Expressway. 'This isn't the way to the airport.'

'No it isn't,' Nick agreed.

'Then where are we going?'

'I just told you,' he said patiently. 'To see my mother.'

'You've got to be kidding.'

'She'll never forgive me if I marry you without bringing you home first.'

'I don't believe this. I have a plane to catch.'

'There will be other planes. We can be married in Phoenix if you want.'

'I want to get out of this car.'

'Not till it stops, please. You might hurt yourself.'

'Nick, this is kidnapping.'

'But it's *my* kid.'

'Very funny. What if I won't agree to marry you?'

'Then I'll introduce you to my father.'

'Your father?'

'When he learns that you're pregnant, he'll murder me if we don't get married. You wouldn't want my demise on your conscience, would you?'

'Nick, you're crazy.'

'Crazy in love with you. You're a slippery fish, but I think I've got you hooked so that you won't get away this time. Do you give up?'

'What will you do if I won't?'

'Keep you on the end of my hook until you say uncle.'

'And if I never do?'

'You will.'

'Oh, will I now?' Kathryn looked back out of the window. She tried to feel angry, insulted, manipulated; but instead she felt inordinately pleased. If Nick was manipulating her, it was only through honesty. He was laying himself wide open to her, and she could hurt him terribly if she chose.

She suddenly realised how much courage it must have taken for him to pursue her in the face of constant rejection. It was the kind of courage only a coward like herself could appreciate.

She looked over at him and noticed for the first time that he was sitting as stiffly as she, and his knuckles were white as he gripped the steering wheel. His words had been so cocky, it hadn't occured to her that he might be as anxious as she about the outcome of his proposal.

Kathryn had been so worried about being hurt herself that she'd never realised that she had as much capacity to hurt a man as he had to hurt her. It was a revelation. She didn't want to harm this man in any way. She loved him.

And to top it off, he came with a ready-made family of parents, sisters, and nieces. She'd never thought about being an aunt, but she liked the idea. She liked the sound of his whole family—including his father.

She looked straight ahead out of the front window, cleared her throat, and tried to say the words that would put them both out of their misery. 'I um . . . I

. . .' Oh, god, could she really say it? She felt as though the bottom had fallen out of her stomach.

She tried again, 'Nick?'

'Yes, I'm still here.' His words were light but she thought she saw a tightening around his mouth as though he were preparing for the worst.

Only *she* could relieve the anxiety that was in him, and fright was blocking her vocal cords. She tried again, but all that came out was a muttered, 'Uncle.'

It was enough. He began to smile and asked, 'What was that?'

'You heard me.'

'But say it again.'

She took a deep breath and said it all, 'Uncle! I love you! I give up!'

'You mean you're actually going to marry me?'

'Do you want me to take it back?'

'Not on your life. Give me a minute to pull off the road and I'll kiss you.'

'I can wait.'

'But I can't . . .' He slid the car into the exit lane and then drove off the highway on to a side road. As soon as the car stopped, he pulled her on to his lap.

Their kiss was long and satisfying and threatened to take them beyond the bounds of what they could do in the confines of the driver's seat. They broke away smiling.

'I love you, I love you, I love you, I love you.' Kathryn couldn't believe how good it was to say the words out loud.

'I know,' Nick returned smugly, 'but I was afraid I was never going to get you to admit it.'

'Would you really have come to Phoenix with me?'

'Or Timbuktu, if necessary,' he agreed.

'And were we really going to see your mother?'

'We still are.'

'Oh.'

'And we'll see *your* mother tomorrow. I made a second set of reservations just in case.'

'You think of everything, don't you?'

'I try to.' He slid a hand between them into his coat pocket and brought out a small box.

Kathryn looked into his eyes and saw that they mirrored the love and delight that was inside her. She took off her glove and watched as he placed the ring upon her finger. He had got her a Christmas present after all.

Mills Boon

Take 4 Exciting Books Absolutely FREE

Love, romance, intrigue... all are captured for you by Mills & Boon's top-selling authors. By becoming a regular reader of Mills & Boon's Romances you can enjoy 6 superb new titles every month plus a whole range of special benefits: your very own personal membership card, a free monthly newsletter packed with recipes, competitions, exclusive book offers and a monthly guide to the stars, plus extra bargain offers and big cash savings.

**AND an Introductory FREE GIFT for YOU.
Turn over the page for details.**

As a special introduction we will send you four exciting Mills & Boon Romances Free and without obligation when you complete and return this coupon.

At the same time we will reserve a subscription to Mills & Boon Reader Service for you. Every month, you will receive 6 of the very latest novels by leading Romantic Fiction authors, delivered direct to your door. You don't pay extra for delivery — postage and packing is always completely Free. There is no obligation or commitment — you can cancel your subscription at any time.

You have nothing to lose and a whole world of romance to gain.

Just fill in and post the coupon today to **MILLS & BOON READER SERVICE, FREEPOST, P.O. BOX 236, CROYDON, SURREY CR9 9EL.**

Please Note:- READERS IN SOUTH AFRICA write to Mills & Boon, Postbag X3010, Randburg 2125, S. Africa.

FREE BOOKS CERTIFICATE

To: Mills & Boon Reader Service, FREEPOST, P.O. Box 236, Croydon, Surrey CR9 9EL.

Please send me, free and without obligation, four Mills & Boon Romances, and reserve a Reader Service Subscription for me. If I decide to subscribe I shall, from the beginning of the month following my free parcel of books, receive six new books each month for £6.60, post and packing free. If I decide not to subscribe, I shall write to you within 10 days. The free books are mine to keep in any case. I understand that I may cancel my subscription at any time simply by writing to you. I am over 18 years of age.

Please write in BLOCK CAPITALS.

Signature _____

Name _____

Address _____

_____ Post code _____

SEND NO MONEY — TAKE NO RISKS.

Please don't forget to include your Postcode.

Remember, postcodes speed delivery. Offer applies in UK only and is not valid to present subscribers. Mills & Boon reserve the right to exercise discretion in granting membership. If price changes are necessary you will be notified.

6R   *Offer expires 31st March 1986.*

EP